WHERE IS MY MIND?

A Book About Depression

A NOVEL BY RYAN SCAGNELLI

Cover by Shannon Greenhaus

GRAPHIC CONTENT AND TRIGGER WARNING

Depression, self-harm and suicide are discussed in detail throughout this book. Please do not read this if you are feeling suicidal or if you are thinking of hurting yourself, instead go to the end of the book where a list of resources is located. Self-harm and suicide are never the answer… take it from a guy to tried both.

CONTENTS

Dancing to a devil's tune. I waltz through fire.

FEAR

I

Home was on his mind. The bittersweet sensation of want and fear clustered and confused his thoughts. He wanted to be back—back in his room, door shut, shades drawn, his favorite book '*Ender's Shadow*' in his lap. He longed for the old-book smell of paper and ink, he wanted to crack his window and let the scent of freshly mowed grass on a hot day sweep into his dark room. He wanted to feel the soft sheets and blankets of his bed against his skin and fall into them, gently entangled like a child swaddled in a blanket—feel that sense of security embedded in being held in a safe and familiar space.

But then there was that fear. Fear of seeing them, his family, speaking to them and being forced to tell them about everything that happened. Being forced to see his mother. He could remember her yells, so vicious and heart-shattering. What would his sister say? His brother? What would his friends say? Being home would take him out of this sanctuary of isolation and into a place where he would have to face more than just his family - he would have to face everyone. He would have to face himself. How could he do that?

His thoughts started to drift, moving back to what happened just a few days before—it seemed like a nightmare or a memory

distorted with age: splintered wood, screams, hot tears and stains of...
He shook his head, trying to push those murky memories out of his
mind. But the pain wouldn't let him escape, wouldn't let him forget
while not letting him see clearly either. Like the silhouette of a monster
lurking.

No, he thought, *just stop it.*

But he couldn't, he saw the door bursting in, the pain traced
through his mind, illuminating a dark path of forgotten feelings.
Repressed shouts and yells cracked like thunder shaking him to the
bones; a silver kiss pressed into his arm, poisoning his mind and heart;
the monster lurking howling with laughter.

All he knew was that he needed to leave, to get out, to escape
this terrible nightmare. To either remember completely or forget
entirely.

He wanted to scream.

Instead, he pushed himself up and off the hospital bed and
walked to the window.

Outside, people walked to and from their cars, navigating a
parking lot that held hundreds of the wheeled metal boxes. A man was
holding his daughter's hand as they strolled through the early light of
the morning and up to the building's main entrance. The girl had light
brown hair and was wearing a yellow sundress. She was holding a
balloon spinning slightly making it difficult to read, but he thought it
said, "Get Better Soon!" with hearts bordering the words. Two other
people, both adults, not holding hands and staying a careful distance
away from each other meandered away from the building and to their
car—a red Jeep—slowly getting in. The car didn't move for a long while.
Eventually, he saw the red brake-lights flash and then turn white as the
reverse lights went. The Jeep gradually pulled out and proceeded
towards the exit.

I wish I were in that car, he thought. *A car with two strangers who didn't want to talk and could take me somewhere, anywhere that wasn't here or home.*

There was a knock on the door followed by the *click* of the latch. "Hello, David," a friendly voice said. "How are you today?"

Dear god, not her again.

David sighed audibly and turned to face down the intruder.

The woman who stood before him looked like she was in her mid to late twenties. She had blonde hair, black-rimmed glasses with light blue eyes residing behind each lens; her face always gave David the impression of being "sharp" and "bright". Today, like every other day for however long he had been there (years it felt like), she had come in, white jacket on, clutching her black clipboard with various sheets of paper and attempted to talk to him.

David absolutely hated her.

She waited expectantly. When he didn't speak, she gave the barest of sighs and smiled.

"How did you sleep?" No response. "I have always loved sleeping in these beds, my partner hates when I stay over though." She looked distractedly out the window. She pulled a pen from her pocket and began tapping it against her chin. "I think it might be because he gets lonely, but I always like to think it's because he just misses me so much. But what can I do when I work nights?" With a shrug she turned back to David.

Cool. Story. Why? Just why?

David stared at her blankly. The woman smiled at him again - it was almost blinding.

Then, even surprising himself, David responded. "I slept like...

3

shit. Thanks for asking. What's your name again?"

She looked at David and blinked.

"Lily," she answered slowly, pursing her lips slightly. She tapped her ID on her jacket. On it, read, "Lily Minette, Residential Psychiatry."

Before she could open her mouth to go on, David spoke again, "This place creeps me out. I feel like I'm part of a horror movie. But, if I'm being honest, the real horror of this place is the smell." He let disdain trickle into his words, not really wanting her to like him. It was easier that way.

Lily blinked again. She turned and examined the room. The walls and ceiling were white as clouds and so was the tiled floor. The bed in the corner which sat across from the window was also white and had two sea-blue pillows on it. She glanced behind her to the door. It was friendly looking, the color of light brown wood. The room was well-lit with plenty of natural light streaming through the window.

She turned back to David and raised an eyebrow. "How exactly does this remind you of a horror movie?" She sniffed the air. "And I don't smell anything." Then she smiled, "Honestly, this place smells better than my apartment, but that's probably because of my partner's cooking. He likes to... take certain culinary risks. I think it's good enough usually."

"Your boyfriend sounds like a real treat." *Seriously,* David thought, *what's up with this girl and her boyfriend. I wonder if he's real...*

Lily's smile broadened and she nodded, "He has his moments." She let out a happy sigh and her eyes glazed over for a second before she refocused them with a blink, "It's so nice to hear you talking! I was getting worried. I'm happy this week of silence is over." A serious look seeped through her enthusiasm.

4

David tried not to roll his eyes. It was true, he had not spoken much over the past couple days or week. When he got here, whenever that was, Lily or whoever would come in and try their best to speak with him. Each and every time they were met with vacant looks and not much else. Lily had gotten used to David's stony silence and soon started "thinking out loud" as she called it whenever she caught herself doing it.

Today, David was putting his foot down because enough was enough.

"Listen, Lily," he said, straightening up and squaring his shoulders, "I think it's time for me to leave. I have taken some time to think and have decided this place," he gestured vaguely to the room they were in, "has given me a good chance to catch my breath, but I need to go." David met Lily's eyes as he finished, trying to appear and sound as confident as he could.

David wasn't sure if he was ready to leave but spending more time here hardly interested him. Stay longer to think about all the terrible shit he did? Pass. Smell this place for another day? Double pass.

Lily's serious expression did not leave her face as she held his gaze. "David," she said, "we all want you to be able to go home, everyone here wants that for you..." she trailed off. "But we can't let you leave until we know that you're okay. There's a process we..."

"Well perfect," David said, cutting her off, "I'm okay, more than okay actually. Can I go? Why don't I call an Uber? May I have my phone back?"

Lily was already shaking her head, "David, it isn't that simple. We need to give you an evaluation, but in order to do so, you need to begin by talking and tell us what happened. You need to talk to me, to us, to anyone. We need to know what exactly happened and we need to know whether it is going to happen again. And if it is, we need to create a plan to help you."

She took a breath and looked briefly at her clipboard, "I know it can be difficult to talk about this stuff. But if you really want to leave then there is a process that we need to follow."

David closed his eyes and turned away. His mask of courage dissolved and he felt waves of fear and frustration rippling through his body. He calmed himself before tears came.

Deep breaths.

When he opened his eyes, he was looking out the window again.

"Lily, I am fine. Why can't you just... I don't know, take my word for it? Please just let me leave this hellish place. I. Am. Fine." He meant to shout, but the last three words were spoken at a whisper.

Lily's voice was soft but clear, "I'm sorry, David. But we can't do that. This is for your own safety."

David continued to stare out the window, trying to comprehend what this person was asking of him.

They want to understand? he thought. *How can I explain it when I don't even understand?*

In a hot flash, anger boiled inside of him, anger at this place, at Lily and at himself.

Before he could respond, Lily spoke again, "The funny thing about saying 'I am fine' is that it almost never means you're fine." She gave David a shrug. "Have you ever seen the movie 'The Italian Job' by chance?" David looked at her, a blank, unreadable expression on his face. "My partner and I watched it the other night. It's one of his favorites. Took him forever to convince me. Well, at the beginning, they define 'Fine' as an acronym that means: freaked out, insecure, narcotic, and emotional." She looked at him, her eyes matched her tone: serious and determined. "It's really easy to say 'I'm fine' but it's a whole other thing to confess that you're freaked out, that you're insecure, that you're narcotic and that you're emotional. It's difficult to be vulnerable, David, but sometimes the only way to make progress and move forward in life is to be just that." She stared at him, letting her words hang in the air.

David opened his mouth, paused, as if to consider his words, and then spoke, "I'm pretty sure it's fucked up."

"What?"

"The 'f' in fine. I've seen the movie. But online it actually says that the 'f' represents 'fucked up.' Pretty sure that whole thing existed before the movie too. They were just borrowing the idea."

"Oh..." Lily said frowning slightly, "Well regardless, you get the point."

"Yes, yes, I get it." He turned away; his gaze being drawn back to the window once again.

Freedom. F is for freedom. How many days have I been trapped in here? he wondered. *It's time to get the hell out.*

"Fine." David said, turning back to Lily, giving her a bitter smile. "Fine. What do you want to know?"

Lily took a step forward, gripping her clipboard just a little tighter. "I want you to explain what happened, David. We just need to make sure that you are okay and that you get the proper support you need to ensure this situation doesn't happen again."

David thought about this and then laughed. It was a sharp joyless laugh that cracked like a whip through the silent room. Sad green eyes looked at Lily, eyes that were tired and grim, the color of dying moss. "I don't even know what happened. No one is going to understand what happened because I don't even understand what happened. I barely even remember! I just want to forget everything and move on with my life!" He finished with his voice raised and filled with frustration. His throat felt rough and raw, hurting from days of not speaking.

Lily's voice was soft, "Sometimes the best way to start understanding something is by talking about it. Just tell me about it, and maybe you'll even start to remember what it is you've forgotten."

David shivered, the idea of telling Lily what happened, the story that so unfairly defined him... it was terrifying, embarrassing.

Vulnerable, he thought, *it was being vulnerable.*

All his life he had prided himself with shrugging off mean jokes, rude comments, people pointing out his insecurities, all that stuff, because it was easier to laugh at them then to face them down. Laughing at his problems made it seem like they weren't real, and made it so he never felt vulnerable, never had to confront the things that tugged and tore at his heart and soul.

And look where that's gotten me. A prisoner in a psych wing of a hospital, he thought dryly.

"Okay." David said, closing his eyes and rubbing his face, the simple movement sent little flares of pain up his left forearm. "Okay, I'll talk." His voice cracked and he winced slightly as his arms fell back down to his lap. "But I don't even know where to begin..." David trailed off.

"How about you start from the beginning?" Lily suggested.

This brought David up short. "The beginning," David said. Though it wasn't a question, it wasn't exactly a statement either. The two words seemed foreign to him, he said them like a person learning a new language, simply repeating some unknown sound for the first time. His mind drifted, seeking this thing called 'the beginning'.

When did it begin? he thought. *When did it all start happening?*

"I guess the beginning could be when I stopped speaking to my friends... no it started before that. Or when I broke up with... no, not that either." David sighed and closed his eyes. He stayed like that for a long, silent minute. Finally, he looked back to Lily. "The only beginning I can think of is the beginning of my senior year. Like... I don't know, the first day. Because I don't remember exactly when 'it' actually started."

"Then why don't we start there?" Lily suggested. "Listen, David. I know that this is scary, that talking about what happened isn't going to be easy or fun. But something you need to understand is that if you are serious about doing this, serious about telling me what happened and are serious about getting out of here, then wanting to help yourself is one of the most fundamental steps in starting the healing process. It's impossible to walk through life without any help, don't misunderstand, David. People need other people, we're social creatures. But I think what makes the biggest difference sometimes is whether or not the person wants to heal. Does that make sense?"

David thought about it and shrugged. "I guess." he said, although he didn't really understand.

"Alright," Lily said, glancing at her watch, "I need to make the rounds but I'll block off some time tomorrow. Due to the circumstance, there shouldn't be any problems. Does that sound good?"

David was relieved that she didn't have time today. "Yeah. Your boss will be happy I'm finally talking."

Lily nodded. "She will be happy you're willing to open up and work with us, yes. As a FYI, I will be contacting my supervisor, and will go over with her everything we've talked about and will be talking about. Just to be completely transparent. I'll probably be required to at least take notes while you are telling me your story."

Lily made a note on her clipboard and tucked her pen into her breast pocket. "Right, I'll be back tomorrow. For now, think, breath, and think some more. Just know that it will be okay. No matter what." She smiled at David one last time, turned and left the room.

As soon as the door shut, silence filled the room. The only noise was David's breathing which only amplified the deafening nothingness.

David sat on the bed for a long while, not blinking, not moving, not doing anything. He simply sat thinking. The idea of facing down what happened to him was petrifying, completely unwanted, but now necessary. He replayed Lily's words in his head, 'You need to want to help yourself.' If that's what it was going to take, then he was going to go all in. If that was the only way to move on, to not only get out of this room, this building, this hospital, but to move on with his life--he was going to do it. He needed to confront and face down what had happened. Face down what he had turned into—the stranger that took over his body and mind. He needed to help himself. He needed to want to help himself. But was he ready?

Lunch came, and then dinner—both meals were picked at, but mostly weren't touched. For the rest of the day, David sat, stood, paced, and laid, thinking about the past year, trying to remember, trying to sift through the dense fog that seemed to conceal and cloud his memories. All the while, Lily's words echoed in his head.

David didn't get much sleep that night, too many thoughts spun and whirled through his mind. His head hurt from all the thinking. Fear in his heart would not let him find rest. On several occasions, tears dampened David's pillow as memories slowly began trickling out, slowly revealing themselves.

In the early hours of the morning, just before the sun's first light warmed and lit the world, David finally drifted away. But even in sleep he found no peace. Images of his friends and the events of that final night haunted his dreams, turning them into terrible nightmares.

Blood, splintered wood, screams, and tears were the first things on his mind when he woke.

II

David showered in the little bathroom that was outside his room and quickly changed into some loose basketball shorts and a plain grey long-sleeved shirt. The familiar smell of detergent reminded him of home, making him long for freedom even more.

David's family had come to see him over the past week, sporadically checking in on him, or at least his sister, brother and Father. He said few words to them, making it clear that he didn't want them to stay. He was just so embarrassed. Humiliated. The sorry looks they gave him cut into him, sharp, piercing and piteous, and he couldn't bear the pain they silently inflicted.

His mother had yet to visit him in the hospital, and he guessed that she wouldn't—not after everything that happened.

Soon breakfast was served. Fruit with a Greek yogurt and a plastic bottle of orange juice. He picked up the yogurt a couple of times, tossing it up and back and forth between hands as he paced around. That was the most he touched his breakfast.

His eyes kept darting towards the door to his room. There were butterflies in his stomach, going wild with anticipation, and each time he heard footsteps outside in the hallway, they would flutter harder, making him feel more and more nauseas. He soon found himself laying on his bed, eyes shut, trying not to think. At 10:30, his waiting finally came to an end.

There was a knock and the door handle clicked. David's eyes flicked open at the sound and he sat up just in time to see Lily walking in. She was slightly out of breath.

"I am so sorry it took me so long to get here!" Lily said, breathing hard. "I treated myself to an exercise class and my partner decided that he would let me make breakfast this morning." She smiled to herself. "It was very sweet. I over-cooked the eggs since I was rushing," Lily chuckled, "but he said they were perfect. Love despite, not because, right?"

"No worries, Lily," David said. He wanted to make a snide remark about her boyfriend but was too distracted.

"Anyways, how has your day been going?" Lily now stood in the center of the room, looking thoughtfully at David. When he didn't respond she added, "What you are doing is very brave, David."

David turned his body so his legs dangled over the bed's side and he pointedly ignored the shallow words of encouragement. "Uh, yeah. Time to start I guess."

Lily walked over to the window and put up the shade—David had put it down in the early hours of the morning in a last-ditch effort to sleep. Sunlight streaked into the room and David winced.

"I'm sure you want to get started. But first, let me find some comfy chairs—I know we keep some in storage, which is right down the hall. I'll go get them."

"Can I help?" David called after her, eager for an excuse to get out of the room, even for a brief instant.

"No, thank you though. Just hold the door when I get back!" Lily called over her shoulder.

David stood; his legs were tight from laying on the bed all morning. He walked to the doorway and looked out. He glimpsed Lily disappearing into a room down the hallway. He sighed, turned back and began to stretch his legs. He bent down, tried to touch his toes, found that he couldn't, but held that position, trying to dive further to the floor. His shirt fell over his head, but he held himself there, counting to ten, feeling like a puppet with its strings cut. When he stood his head swam a little, but once it cleared, he found himself feeling a little better.

He adjusted his shirt and looked back down the hallway. He almost laughed when he saw Lily pulling an armchair that was about the size of her. David stepped into the hallway, walked to her and started pulling. Lily was about to object, but once she saw how quickly the chair slid with both of them, she smiled and abstained from any protests.

"Thanks for the help."

Soon, David and Lily were sitting in the room, both in armchairs facing each other.

"Well, shall we?" Lily asked.

"Um, yes..." David said slowly. He opened his mouth, then closed it, then opened it, and then closed it. Finally, he said, "Sorry, I'm a bit... uh."

Lily, who had been waiting patiently smiled gently, "There is no need to be nervous. I know what you're about to tell me is personal and scary. I know." She and David looked at each other, eyes locked. "This is a safe place, David. It will be okay." David looked away from her and to the window he so often gazed out of.

A long silence was drawn between them.

Still staring out the window, David spoke, "I've been thinking a lot about this, all day yesterday. All night. All morning. Some things have come back to me, other things haven't. Last week, that final night, and a lot leading up to it I still can't remember. I still don't even know how I ended up here." He paused and looked at Lily. "But," he continued, "I do know where to start. Yesterday you were right, I think I need to start at the beginning. The beginning of my senior year. Before anything happened. That way I think I'll be able to remember things, then I'll just push forward and through…" His voice was quiet and his eyes distant when he trailed off.

"Sounds like a good strategy," Lily said approvingly. "Also, you should be happy to hear that I have been authorized to begin the process of your transition back home—if I think you're ready for it. I am required to take notes, so I hope that my scribbling won't distract you too much. Also, these notes will be shared with your parents." She tapped her clipboard with her pen.

David sighed. "Thanks for letting me know. Uh, so yeah, I think it's time for me to convince you to let me get the hell out of here."

"Let's not get ahead of ourselves, David. Let's start slowly. Why don't we get through today and see where we're at? Tell me what you're comfortable with but try to be as honest as you can. And before you dive right into it, could you tell me a little bit about your high school? Set the scene if you will."

David shrugged, "Sure. Let's get this over with. To the beginning we go."

THE BEGINNING

I

It's strange. What happened my senior year, I think, was the most important thing that has happened to me in my 18 years. Not only that, but whether I like it or not, I realize that it was probably the most defining thing of my life so far, and perhaps, will be the most defining thing of my entire life. And right now, since I'm supposed to be honest, it's the thing that I am most humiliated by, the thing that terrifies me most of all, and something that will stay with me forever. I still don't understand what happened, and I don't think I'll ever fully understand. For what happened, the thing that took control of me was subtle, cunning and insidious, and in the end, almost stole my life away.

With that being said, I'll start with my senior year and the very first day of classes. It's funny to think that my friends and I thought we were going to be the Kings and Queens of the school, that it would be the perfect year to end our high school careers, that we were unstoppable and invincible, as all seniors do. But as you may have guessed, we were wrong.

A brief description of my high school follows as such:

Regardless of any general predispositions you may have about high school, mine will for the most part disprove them. For the most part. There's still drama, romance, tears and all your typical high school stuff. However, there are no stereotypical bullies that roam around the halls, shoving undeserving freshmen into lockers as they try to sneak past unnoticed. There are no mean girls who humiliate others in public places just for sport. There were mean people, bullies, whatever you want to call them, all places everywhere have them, but as a whole, my school is pretty friendly—albeit white as hell.

In my school, the popular kids are the smart ones. Intelligence had taken over. Popular kids had the highest GPA's and usually were dual or even triple-athletes. We were competitive, from grades to sports, SAT scores to chess in the library. Our school embodied the idea of 'work hard, play hard' and even our intellectual elites occasionally found themselves running from the cops busting a party.

There is much, much more to my school, but for the sake of my story I will leave it at that since that's all you need to know. It really was a good school, with nice people and caring teachers. But now I'm not sure I'll be ever able to go back there, to face those hallowed halls and the people walking through them.

I have (or maybe had at this point) two best friends. Leland (Lee for short) and Charlie (Charlie for short). Both are amazing in their own ways, and both are crazy smart. Smartest people I've ever known. Ever since we became best friends, I have been their bad influence and in turn, they were my good ones. I would pull them into trouble and try to corrupt them as best as I could, and they were always there to pull me out of whatever mess I made.

***

"Ready?" David asked.

Lily gave David an encouraging nod. "Ready."

***

16

It was a beautiful day, the sun shining, a warm breeze gently blowing. I was driving to school, for the first day of classes of my senior year and had Jimmy Buffett's *Cheeseburger in Paradise* blasting. Being the responsible vegetarian that I was, I replaced "Cheeseburger" with "Beanburger" on each chorus. Steph, my little sister was riding shotgun and was trying to conceal her identity as best she could. With the middle school right across the street, Steph rode to school with me sometimes. Today she had been complaining loudly that I was going to make her late.

As I pulled into the high school's parking lot, Steph opened the door and jumped out of the still moving car, heading quickly for the middle school. I laughed at her embarrassment of being seen in public with me and parked my car.

"My man!" Charlie was walking away from his dad's old red Buick and towards me. He had a fresh haircut—his black hair had been buzzed into a short mohawk of sorts— and was dressed to impress, wearing blue jeans (despite the heat) and a perfectly ironed white buttoned down with the sleeves rolled up. He looked like a pubescent nerdy James Bond villain. Clearly the first day of classes was something he had been looking forward to. "I still can't believe that still runs," he called out, gesturing to my car. His dark brown eyes sparkled and he gave me a smirk.

I laughed, parked and got out, sling my backpack over one shoulder. I glanced back. It was by dad's old 1995 Cutlass Supreme Oldsmobile Convertible. It sat in the late summer sun, top still down, its chipped green paint warming contently.

"This baby is beautiful and is better than anything you'll ever own!" I called to Charlie as he made his way to me.

Charlie reached me, clapped me on the back, and directed us both to the entrance of our school. "Your Dad got that thing off Ebay, and it's as old as you are. Steph was in a hurry, huh?"

"And? That just makes it vintage. Or young... Old? Whatever! It should be in a showroom." I said. Both of us laughed. "And yeah, she didn't want to be late. What a nerd." I let out a long breath. "Well, this is it. Senior year, baby. Our time to shine. Nice haircut by the way. Trying to make the ladies swoon on the first day?"

"I figured I better be looking good for the beginning of the end," he said and gave me one of his classic 'Charlie smiles'—perfect white teeth, sparkling eyes, just the barest hint of dimples on each of his cheeks. Honestly, it almost made me swoon. "You haven't heard anything about the end of the summer party, have you?" He sighed. "I heard it was crazy. My parents had me double and triple checking all the summer homework due. Still can't believe teachers are giving seniors work over the summer. It's like they're reminding us that they still have a year to torment us."

"We had homework?!" I asked incredulously. "For which classes?!" I groaned and smacked my forehead. "My parents knew they should have grounded me for something. They just didn't know what for."

"Dave, if you get grounded again, I'm gonna kill you. At least don't get your phone taken away for a year again."

"I still have the essay I wrote to get it back," I snorted. "I'll just have to write an essay about how I forgot to write other essays."

We approached the double wide doors, pushed them open and walked into the main lobby of the school. It was a big square room, with cushioned benches framing the "senior carpet" which sat directly at its center. No underclassmen were allowed on it. To the right, stairs went down to the cafeteria area and up to the gym. To the left, hallways, classrooms, stairs to more classrooms and all the administration offices. Everything was decorated in blue and gray, our school colors.

We stopped and scanned the packed crowd. The entire senior class (all 200 of us) seemed to be here, talking (more like yelling) and catching up. After a moment of searching, I found what I was looking for. I cupped my hands over my mouth and yelled, "Lee! Leland!" Leland's back was turned to us, she was talking with a group of other seniors, but I recognized the classic brunette ponytail she always wore. At my yells, she turned and saw Charlie and me. Despite this, I began jumping up and down, waving my arms frantically in the air, "Leland! We're over here! Lee! Leland!"

A chorus of heckles from familiar faces called out from the lobby before us, saying, "Oh shut up, David!" and "Look who's back!" and other things along those lines. I only smiled and waved at them. Charlie just rolled his eyes and watched as a now annoyed Leland pushed her way through the crowd towards us.

"Garraway!" A gravelly voice called out. It was Mr. Meyers, an ancient man, responsible for signing in students that arrived late to school. His desk sat directly in front of the entrance. His spotted face was wrinkled and resembled old dried-out leather. All of this was accompanied by his usual blue polo and loose khaki pants only held up by a belt. He shook his head and angrily called out, "For Christ's sake, it's the first day of class. Wanna get written up your first damn minute back?"

I turned and smiled broadly at him. He and I were awfully familiar with each other at this point. Being late to school was one of the few things I excelled at.

"Where's your school spirit, Mr. Meyers? Aren't you happy class is back in session?"

"Must have forgot it at home," he muttered dryly and turned to Charlie. "Charlie," he croaked, "you have a nice vacation?"

Charlie, who had never once gotten on Mr. Meyers' bad side, smiled and said, "I did Mr. Meyers! It's good to be back."

And with that, Mr. Meyers nodded and continued to watch the

front doors from his little desk, craning his neck to glare at any voice or noise he deemed too loud, which today was everyone.

Leland, who was wearing a red shirt tucked into white shorts, reached us and crossed her arms, "Already being written up on the first day, David? Serves you right." She glared through her glasses with familiar but intense blue eyes.

Ignoring her comment, Charlie and I both laughed and wrapped our arms around her.

"I thought the two of you were going to be late this morning. The audacity!" She pushed us off her and threw her arms up.

"I was thinking about it," I grinned. "Make a statement on the first day of school. Almost did too. Steph didn't want to though." Charlie and Leland only rolled their eyes at me and then both cracked smiles.

"Another point for Team Queen." Leland remarked. She said this or a variation of this every time a clear example of, as she usually explained it as, 'how women are smarter and therefore superior' exposed itself. "And David, no one wants to ride with you if you're only going to play Jimmy Buffet--which I assume you were playing."

I barked a laugh. "Come on," I said ignoring her, "Let's see 'em! Who has what?"

Before anyone could show their class schedule, Leland blurted, "I have AP physics, then AP calc, then AP Spanish, and then SLAM to finish off the day. Those are my gray days. I know all of us are in SLAM, because obviously. Also, David, aren't you in AP physics this year?"

"Yes I am," I said proudly, handing Charlie my schedule and taking Leland's. "Should be a good time too. I hear Mr. Ellis is pretty easy."

"We're all in AP physics together," Charlie noted.

"Thank god for that," I said.

Leland pursed her lips. "As long as you two aren't too distracting, it will be fine. Also, we'll need to be in lab groups together, if Ellis gives us grief just leave it to me. I carried us last year in the debate. That man owes me."

Charlie chuckled, "Like we have choice, or Ellis himself for that matter. Should be a pretty cool semester. I hope David explodes something like he did last year in Chem." I rolled my eyes and snorted. Charlie smiled at Leland. "Lee, you and I are in AP Calc together too."

"Ah yes, well let me know if you have a hard time keeping up." Leland said playfully, winking at Charlie. Leland knew that Charlie was a wiz with numbers and could out math her any day of the week. Which isn't to say she wouldn't get a perfect grade in the class this year too.

"German 3, huh Dave?" He smirked. "Still don't know why you didn't take Spanish with us."

"German is a cool language," I shrugged. "Ich spreche schlect. I hope the two of you enjoy your Spanish and advanced calc, along with the rest of your other advanced placement classes. Nerds."

We continued to exchange schedules until the bell rang and we all turned. The lobby was now chaos, with students running, laughing, pushing and hugging. Familiar and friendly faces swam and rushed by in the current of bodies. Slowly, it started to clear out as they made their way to their first period.

Leland grabbed us by the arms and directed Charlie and I towards the science wing, "Come on, don't want to be late. Let's go!"

And so, the three of us went to our Physics class. After, we split up, heading in different directions. My second class was World Affairs with Mr. Kelly, and after that German 3 with Herr Luce. They both flew by since the teachers were doing the bare minimum—as it was the very first class. After they presented the syllabus to us, they mostly let us catch up with our fellow classmates, promising us that on our next Grey Day they would begin formal classes and 'actual learning' would take place.

Finally, it was fourth period and time for our SLAM class. SLAM, an acronym for: Student, Leadership, Advisement, and Membership. I wasn't entirely thrilled about this last class, but then again I wasn't dreading it either. It was more of a program than anything, placing an incoming group of freshmen with three seniors during their homerooms on Thursdays and Fridays. There wasn't any homework and it looked good on a college application since not all seniors were accepted into it.

Our teacher, Mrs. Randolph had been in charge of this class and program for over ten years—something she gently reminded students every time there was a "crisis" and would show them how to handle and resolve each in turn. She had a good reputation. When she talked to you, she was completely perceptive, you could feel her listening with all of her attention, and she could actually understand you when you were unable to put certain feelings or thoughts into words. She was almost everyone's favorite teacher.

Over the summer, the seniors selected for SLAM were gathered for a retreat that lasted one weekend, during which we were placed into our SLAM groups. That's where a lot of us really got to know Mrs. Randolph. Lee had talked her way into getting what she wanted per usual, and once again Charlie, Lee and I found ourselves placed together. It wasn't very surprising. Lee wasn't the Captain of the debate team for nothing.

When I walked into the classroom, Leland and Charlie were already there sitting next to each other on the far side of the room. Most of the class was already there. There were no desks, instead a big circle of chairs took up almost the whole room, this way, one could see every other person in the room from any of the chairs.

"Good afternoon, David. Welcome to your first day of SLAM!" Mrs. Randolph said cheerfully, greeting me with a warm smile. She stood by the door, as if she were planning on greeting each and every person who showed up. "Please sit with your fellow SLAM leaders."

"Hey Mrs. Randolph, you got it." I said, giving her a thumbs-up and walking over to an empty seat between Charlie and a girl named Lena Wellburns. I said hello to Lena and turned to catch up with Charlie and Leland.

"How we doing?" I asked both of them. Charlie shrugged, telling me that it was a boring first day of classes. Leland on the other hand, dove into a great description of her classes, explaining each syllabus, how grades were weighted and what that meant in terms of priorities for her and time allocation this coming semester. Charlie gave me a look that told me he had heard this already and/or lived it, but he let her go on and nodded along as if it was the first time hearing it.

When Mrs. Randolph was ready to begin, she placed herself in the last remaining seat and held up her right hand in the "quiet coyote" sign. Her pointer finger and pinkie fingers were up in the air and her thumb, middle and ring fingers all pressed together, making a vague impression of a coyote's head. It was simple but effective, shown by how quickly the room fell silent.

"Welcome to our very first class of the year. I want to start by saying how proud I am of all of you for doing well during this summer's training and I am very excited to see how well you do throughout this year." Her voice was soft and relaxing, and she smiled at each of us in turn. "Today, we are going to begin by doing some icebreakers. I know you all must be a little frazzled by the prospect of a new year, new classes, perhaps the idea of college in the very near future, but I want this classroom to be a sanctuary and a safe space to you all. I want this classroom to welcome happy thoughts and dissuade all the stress of the outside world.

"With that being said, we will be learning and planning at the same time. We will meet here in this classroom or if it's a nice day perhaps outside. We're scheduled for Mondays, Wednesdays and Fridays during gray weeks and the Tuesdays and Thursdays for blue weeks. We will usually begin our class with an icebreaker and a mindfulness activity so we can ground ourselves in this room and connect with each other. Then, we will discuss your freshmen groups— how they're doing, any problems, successes, and future plans with them. Our job this year is to integrate them into our school's community by first getting them to open up to each other, then giving them the courage to explore the facilities within our entire school. We want them to be comfortable with getting to classes and going out for sports teams or clubs. A lot of you are involved with almost all of our teams, clubs, and so on. You are going to be their role models, so be conscious of everything you say and do when in your homerooms. On non-SLAM days, Monday through Wednesday, you will simply be there, present in your assigned homerooms, available to them. They will probably complete homework and socialize, but I want you to show them that you are there, not just physically. I know it sounds like a lot, but you'll soon find out for yourselves that it can be a piece of cake. So, let's get started."

II

When I got home and walked into my house, I was met by my mom sitting at the kitchen table. She was wearing her favorite navy-blue shirt with black work pants, her light chestnut hair fell just below her shoulders and swayed slightly as she typed on her laptop.

She looked up and smiled, "Hey, honey. How was school?" She asked excitedly. "Fun first day?"

"It was fine. It's gonna be a busy semester but should be

alright."

"Well that's good to hear! When do cross-country practices start up? You'll have to give Dad and I your race schedule."

I had told my parents offhandedly that I might be thinking about joining the cross-country team since so many of my friends were on it (i.e. Charlie and Leland) but I didn't think I was going to race. I was leaning towards only practicing with them after school—just for something to do and to stay in shape.

"Next week, I think. I don't know, soon. And I think I'm only practicing with them. I don't really want to be on the actual team and compete. Don't really want to embarrass myself, yah know?"

"David, you would do great! Where is your confidence?"

I shrugged the question off, grabbed some food out of the fridge and headed towards the hallway leading upstairs.

"David!" my mom called after me, stopping me short. "Come back and talk to me. Tell me about your classes. I want to hear about them!"

"Mom, it was the first day, nothing happened," I said, turning to look at her. She wore an expression of genuine enthusiasm and curiosity that only a mother can produce over such a mundane thing as school. At my words, she deflated slightly. I sighed. "I promise I'll tell you all about them once things start actually happening."

"Thank you, honey," she smiled contently and looked back to her work.

When I got upstairs, I opened my laptop and scrolled through Facebook, unsure of what to do. Luckily, my phone started buzzing. I looked down to see Charlie calling me.

"What's up?"

"Yo man, fire at Lee's tonight. Want me to pick you up?"

***

"Hold on, David," Lily interrupted. David stopped speaking and looked at Lily. "Can you tell me more about your relationship with your mother?" Lily asked. "Just so I can have a point of reference."

"Oh... Uh, yeah sure." David said.

***

She was a busy person, with basically running our family, making sure everyone was where they were supposed to be, taking care of any and every problem that came up and everything else a mom does—which was a lot, as she liked to remind all of us frequently. On top of that, she was starting her own business, adding to the mountain of work she already was constantly climbing.

Her go-to phrase for when she was irritated with me was, "Where did I go wrong?" She always said it sarcastically but her frustration with me was always there. And I understood why she was always frustrated with me. She constantly told me I was smart, that I had potential to do something. But time and time again, my bad grades, poor decisions, and general stupidity wore her down, made her upset. She thought I wasn't trying hard enough, that I was failing at life on purpose. I was just doing me.

Beyond the point of frustration was the danger zone—typically where I would end up grounded for varying amounts of time or get my phone taken away for too-long periods of time. That's where the rare shouting match might take place but that was the worst it would get.

When I was younger, she would always read to me out loud. She got me hooked on books and ever since I could read for myself, they were my escape, my solace--you know how the cliché goes. I remember one of my favorite books she read to me, can't even remember what it was called, but it something having to do with an intergalactic hunger games inside a library—It blew my mind.

***

"And I know that she loves me, or loved me…" David blinked and a tear from each eye streamed down his cheeks. "Damn, sorry. I've barely started and I'm already crying."

"David, it's okay," Lily said gently. "Why don't you tell me more about your family?"

David nodded and wiped his face again.

***

My brother is named Greg. He's two years older than me and is the golden child of the family. He's gotten straight A's since middle school and he wants to be a doctor. I barely know what I want to eat for breakfast each morning. Being compared to him constantly made me dislike him and not only that, but he and I shared a bedroom until he left for college which didn't exactly help our relationship. We were always arguing with each other, keeping each other up late at night, whispering and fighting over the smallest of things.

My dad's name is Bill, and everyone tells me all of the time that I look a lot like him. The man is a hard worker. The only time I don't see him working is when we visit Florida for vacation. But even when driving there, he was always on his laptop, typing away, sending emails, and answering phone calls. When we weren't on vacation, he worked from home in his office which doubled as our guest room. When he wasn't doing work, he was doing home improvements and I was always recruited. I knew how to tile a floor, put drywall up, fix the holes my brother and I made in the drywall. He taught me a lot.

My sister, Steph, is younger than me by four years. We got a lot closer when my brother left for college. We usually just sat in the same room and just... would be there, in the same space. Talking wasn't usually necessary for us. Our company was enough. Back when Greg was home, they got along pretty well. We had a much different relationship from her and Greg's. They were always talking and laughing.

Steph and Greg did fight sometimes but that's just what family does. My parents fighting, me fighting with my parents, me fighting with my siblings. You know. All the combinations. But me and my mom most of all.

***

"How's that?" David asked.

"Good," Lily said, scribbling down a note. "Now, before you go on, just remember that you don't have to tell me everything that happened to you during your senior year, only the important parts and only what's relevant. Why don't we focus on transitional periods, parts in the story where things begin to change? Those will be the important parts. That sound okay?"

"I'll try my best."

THE STRANGER

I

It wasn't until the first cross-country meeting when things started to get relevant. It happened at the end of the second week of school. By then, classes were in full swing and teachers were dishing out enough homework for everyone to drown in. Students, such as myself but unlike Charlie and Leland, were already eager to focus our energy on anything else.

I arrived at the first meeting. I still wasn't sure if I wanted to be a full member on the team, but Leland had been trying her best to persuade me.

I found Charlie and Leland standing in the far-left area of the school's lobby talking to some friends. Aside from the slowly gathering group of cross-country people, no other students were there since it was 6PM on a Friday night--even Mr. Meyer's desk was vacant. I made my way to them and joined in on their conversation, catching up with some people I still hadn't seen. All the while I avoided Leland's verbal traps to convince me to fully join the team.

When the meeting began, the growing pool of people held about 40 students, the two coaches (one for the women's team and one for the men's), and a few other faculty members who helped out with coordination and supervision of both teams.

It was Coach Torrance, a tall guy resembling Shaggy from "Scooby-Doo" and the head coach of the men's team who spoke first.

"Hello!" he boomed. The general noise of talking students, laughs and shuffling feet came to a stop. "Welcome to another year of cross-country!" He raised his hands up in celebration. His red messy hair tumbled about with the gesture, and a cheer and scattered claps went through the crowd of students and faculty. When everyone settled down again, he continued, "Please, everyone take a seat. I want you to be able to see me and I want to be able to see all of you." Everyone sat. "I'm Coach Torrance, and as many of you know, this," he gestured to the serious-looking woman standing beside him, "is Coach Grosh. We have been coaching this team for about 5 years a piece now, and we cannot be more pleased with the teams both of us are looking at for this coming season!"

I was supposed to be paying attention but I realized that while sitting down I could see most of everyone fairly well, or at least the backs of them. My curiosity for the other students took control. The coach's voice faded to a distant echo and instead, the faces of those around me consumed my attention. I saw Jason Prat (decent runner), Michaela Wassick (best female runner we've had in years), Elly Bartlet (familiar face), Julie Farvoe, Mike Glundy. I continued to scan and after a few more minutes of scanning and looking, I saw a new face, a face I had never seen before.

I nudged Leland with my elbow, "What?" She asked quietly through the corner of her mouth, not looking at me.

"Who's that?" I whispered, nodding in the direction of the unfamiliar face.

Leland glanced in the same direction. "Who's who?" she whispered back, sounding annoyed.

"Over there!" I pointed discreetly without lifting my arm.

"David, who the hell are you pointing to?! Just leave me alone, I'm trying to listen."

I rolled my eyes, smiled with frustration and gave up all effort of subtly. "Her!" I half whispered, half laughing and I lifted my arm and pointed to the girl. Leland looked and made an "ooh" sound, but before she could respond, Coach Torrance stole my attention back.

"You have a question, David?" Though this was the first time I had been to a cross-country practice, Coach Torrance knew me quite well ever since I had taken his driver's ed class my sophomore year.

I froze, realizing my hand was just high enough to seem like a raised hand, or more realistically, Coach Torrance noticed me not paying attention and wanted to have some fun.

"I was..." I sputtered out, unable to come up with anything, anything at all that would justify me pointing at a person while he was talking. Everyone in the room had turned to look at me. Charlie smiled as he began shaking his head and Leland attempted to muffle her laughter.

"Well, even though I was just about to discuss the practice schedules, I see that you are eager to start introducing our new teammates. And sure, let's start with Eva, since you're pointing at her." His eyes sparkled with satisfaction; he knew he had me.

My face turned red as everyone in the room looked from me to the unfamiliar face I was pointing to. *Still pointing to!* I realized and dropped my hand down and flushed even further.

"Eva," Coach Torrance said encouragingly, "why don't you stand and introduce yourself to our team?"

Despite my embarrassment, I looked up at her and what I saw reaffirmed why I had pointed to her to begin with. She looked like a goddess standing above all of us. She wasn't tall but her presence commanded attention. She had black hair with two warrior's braids that fell down her back, tracing her shoulder blades. Strands that escaped those tightly bound coils floated like a midnight halo above her head. Her brown eyes were deep mocha swirls, and freckles artfully covering her face.

She looked over the students sitting down, everyone was now completely focused on her. Her eyes swept the room until they fell on me. My face flushed again to an impossible red as those dark chocolate eyes locked with mine. I gave her a weak smile, and to my despair, she frowned and looked away.

"Hello everyone," she voiced, turning to face the general direction of the crowd. "My name is Eva, as Coach Torrance already said. And... well I'm new." She let loose a nervous chuckle, "I'm a junior and I guess I'm just excited to be a part of your team. So, thanks for letting me be a part of this."

She had a good voice. Whatever that means.

Coach Grosh clapped her hands which prompted claps throughout the crowd—primarily led by the male students. Charlie clapped slowly, smiling at me as he did so.

I clapped my hands twice and stopped, still shaken by that frown she gave me—and my overall embarrassment. It occurred to me that being new here, she probably didn't want the attention that I inadvertently given her. I swore silently under my breath. Leland and Charlie snickered and whispered, "good job" and "smooth," but I ignored them. While they were eating this up, the terrible thought that the cute new girl already hated me sent despair through my body.

"Thank you, Eva." Coach Torrance said. "Moving on. David, who would you like to introduce next?" I closed my eyes as my friends around me began laughing and clapping.

After the meeting, I looked desperately for Eva. To put it simply, I wanted to apologize for being an ass. Leland and Charlie wished me luck and made several more jokes about me messing up and having zero game, and then departed. I searched the slowly dwindling crowd, the students, my peers, moved like flowing water, the doors to the main entrance acted as the mouth of a river, casting those who got too close out into the darkening night.

I turned, looked, turned again, searched, and finally, when I was about to give up, I found Eva was standing right in front of me. She was frowning.

"Hi," I said weakly, trying my best to look as innocent as possible.

"Thanks for that during the meeting. David, was it?" I could see a heat, a small flickering anger in her eyes and I gulped.

"Look, I am really sorry. I was only pointing at you because..." I trailed off, realizing I had no idea what I was actually going to say.

"Because?" She asked, raising an eyebrow.

I laughed nervously, feeling my face begin to flush once more, "Uh..."

Just as I was about to blubber and embarrass myself even further, I felt an arm go around my shoulder, and a very familiar voice finished my sentence.

"Because," Charlie said, chiming in, "he had no idea who the cute new girl was. And my man here wouldn't sit still until he found out."

Charlie could be quite bold when it came to embarrassing me. I looked down at my feet despite myself, but then pushed Charlie off and turned to him.

"I thought you left! Slash, please leave."

"Why would we leave?" Leland laughed, walking over now. "How could Charlie and I miss this? We love seeing you embarrass yourself in front of people. What a gift this meeting has been."

I turned back to Eva, who, while witnessing my friends grind salt into my wound of humiliation, was smirking at them. "Uh... so these are my best friends. Beginning to question why we are friends at all, but... Charlie, this is Eva." I gestured to Lee, "And Eva, this is the lovely Leland. They're as charming as--"

Leland cut me off, "Oh come off it, David. This is us saving you. Be thankful."

"A glass of wine and a fudge brownie?" Charlie suggested. "Damn, that actually sounds pretty good."

"You don't even like wine, Charlie. You just want to eat brownies." Leland snorted, shaking her head at both of us. She looked back at Eva, "Very nice to meet you."

Eva reached and shook both of their hands. She met my eyes once more and to my relief, that small anger I saw before was gone. I could tell that she still wasn't thrilled with me, but at least she wasn't mad.

"Nice to meet you both." Eva said, giving them a warm smile. "What year are you two?"

"Well, all three of us," Leland said, "are seniors." She liked to remind people that the three of us, for better or worse, were a package deal. "And you're a junior? What brings you here? I heard you're from somewhere in New York. Is that true? Where exactly?"

"I am, actually. How did you know?" Eva looked thoughtfully at Lee.

34

"Jesus, Lee." I said, "I thought you didn't know who she was? Can we limit ourselves to one question at a time? Also why are you actually back?"

"As you ask three of your own. The hypocrisy." Lee rolled her eyes at me. "I do know who you are, I have my sources," she said, smiling at Eva, "but I couldn't see where the hell you were pointing David. You suck at pointing apparently. And we're back because of Charlie."

I scoffed as dramatically as possible and then remembered Eva was standing right there and tried to transform it into an awkward shoulder roll which probably looked weird if anything. "Well, leave again please. And I do say this from the bottom of my heart."

Charlie turned and started pulling Leland away. "I forgot to tell Coach he owes me 100 burpees. Ran over 100 miles this summer. That man's gonna be FIT." He smiled and winked. "But yes, David, I think that's our cue. It's time for us to go. For real this time." He looked at Eva, "Really nice meeting you! Don't be too hard of David, I think he likes you."

"Oh, come on! I just want to get to know her!" Lee protested as Charlie guided her away.

I felt the color from my face drain away at Charlie's words and my head felt light and airy.

Eva waved goodbye to Charlie and Lee, "Nice meeting you too."

As they walked away, I heard Charlie say, "Apparently, you already know her. Did you say something about brownies? I could eat."

"You said something about brownies, Charlie." Leland said, shaking her head. And then they were gone.

I turned back to Eva, trying to shake off the endless embarrassment. "So, I am so sorry. Really not how I thought this would

35

be going."

She raised an eyebrow again, "And how did you think this would be going?"

I laughed nervously, "Uh... well not like this. I am so sorry about the meeting. Apparently, I'm not as subtle as I think I am... I just saw you and..."

"And?"

I paused, trying to figure out how to best phrase what I really wanted to say. "I wanted to know who you were." Eva looked at me for a long moment. I couldn't tell what she was thinking.

Good? Bad? She hates me. She absolutely hates me. I began to spiral.

Just then, the quiet but smart junior, Hannah Williams, shuffled over. "Hey, Eva." She looked at me. "Hi David." She turned back to Eva, "I'm gonna head out, do you want a ride?"

Before I knew what I was saying, the words fell out of my mouth, "I could give you a ride." Both Hannah and Eva looked at me. I gave them an innocent smile. "I mean, it's really not a big deal. My car is here. I mean in the parking lot out there." I pointed dumbly in the direction of the only parking lot at the school.

Eva almost smiled. Almost.

"Thanks, but I think I'll go with Hannah." She and Hannah turned and began walking away. My heart sank. But then I saw Eva turn back. For the first time that night, for the first time ever, she smiled at me. It was playful and perfect. "It was almost nice meeting you, David." And she too vanished into the night.

***

Lily put her hand up. "Let's pause for a moment."

David shrugged and sat back in his chair.

"How do you feel after that encounter with your cross-country coach?"

David thought about it and casually said, "Fine. I messed around all of the time in class so I was used to getting called out for my insubordinations." David smiled, "SAT word right there." He thought for a moment, then the smile faded and vanished.

Lily nodded and looked down at her notes. "I am failing to see how this person, Eva, had anything to do with your depression." She looked back up to David with one eyebrow raised.

"Well, it will all make sense when I finish telling the story. But if I'm gonna to be honest, I don't think she had anything to do with what happened. She was just an innocent bystander who got caught up in a mess." David paused and thought for a moment. "Well that's not true. She was involved. I just feel so terrible. It will make sense if I just go on."

"Well, if you say she is important, then she is. After that first... interesting encounter with her, what happened?"

LOVE AND MEMORIES

I

After that first interesting encounter with Eva, operation "Get-her-to-not-hate-me-at-the-very-least" was a go. After that not so great first impression I needed to set a new and ideally better first impression. Or, well second impression. She, being a junior, was difficult to track down during the day. Over the next couple of weeks, I caught glimpses of her every so often but every time I did run into her she was in a hurry or surrounded by new friends. Not only that, but because she was a transfer every boy saw her as new and mysterious not to mention cute as hell. I tried to find out which parties she went to but it didn't seem like she went to any.

Even my friends and I went to the occasional party (I typically had to force Leland and Charlie). We would blow off some steam, take some shots, drink bad beer and pretend we didn't have better things to be doing. But eventually, we would remember those better things and always dragged ourselves back to reality in the morning, through a molasses-thick hangover—when everything seemed to take extra effort.

The one place I knew I could find her was at the beginning of cross-country practice. Our boy's and girl's teams would stretch and warmup together and then separate—the coaches finding new and exciting exercises to torture/train us with. The boy's team, myself included, was more interested in flirting with the girl's team than actually stretching. During stretches and before practice started, I would go out of my way to talk to Eva. At this point, the boys team knew I had a huge crush on her and for most of them. Thankfully, the air of mystery that came with her transfer had lifted, and so their attentions wandered elsewhere--typically to their old intrigues.

For the first couple times, all I did was apologize, blabber, stumble over words, and continue to embarrass myself. On several occasions, Charlie and Leland had to come save me.

Then, I finally began to make progress. I gained the ability to talk to her and not embarrass myself, to speak coherently and sometimes even intelligently. I began to make her laugh and smile. We mostly talked about classes and cross-country practices since that's pretty much the only things we had in common at the time. Then, one practice I caught her alone, built up the courage to ask for her number and, to my surprise, got it. I asked if I could buy her coffee.

In all my years, I've learned that coffee is the best first date. If you're serious about the person, don't go to the movies, don't go bowling, don't bring them to a party. Not for the first real date at least. Coffee is perfect because it is simple but meaningful. You sit, you talk, you spend about three bucks—perfect. On top of that, you actually get to know the person. With other dates, something is distracting you from each other. With coffee, you get to experience the other person, hear them, see them, really get to know them, and perhaps, if you're lucky, begin to understand them. And then there's the smell. There's something about a small little coffee shop smell, its aroma, its complex simplicity that comforts, relaxes and focuses—let's people talk freely.

We met at such a place; a shop called "Hidden Grounds." It was my favorite coffee shop in town. It was small, romantically lit, all the furniture was made of dark glazed wood, strung dried flowers framed each doorway and the stone walls had all kinds of nooks and crannies.

For years and years, people had hidden small folded notes in the cracks of the walls, on which were words of encouragement, quotes from their favorite authors, a good joke, premonitions that could leave you wondering, or, if you got lucky, a stranger's secret.

It was late in the morning on a crisp Saturday and as I walked through the comfortable, almost perfect fall air I could feel my palms sweating. Was I nervous? Absolutely. I couldn't remember anything from when Eva and I talked at cross country practices. All my dumb boy brain remembered was how cute she is, and how smart.

Then there was the profound sensation of uncertainty that comes with going on a date. They're so simple, just straightforward human interaction, but at the same time, there is so much at stake—or at least it seemed that way. What should you say? What shouldn't you say? What stupid things will you inevitably say? It was terrifying and exciting all at once.

The pressure was getting to me and I started to go over every single insecurity and personal flaw that I was aware of. The vest probably looked stupid, I definitely looked fat, and what if I puked on the table because I was so nervous? Dear God, what if I puked on her? Scenarios of me puking on her and the table started running through my mind; how she would probably never want to see or speak to me ever again, how she would tell the school and I would probably have to move—change my name too just to be safe. I began to regret eating such a large breakfast that morning. Would my scrambled eggs make a second appearance today?

As I walked up to the cozy coffee shop, all I could think about was that frown Eva gave me when we first met. I thought about it often--it persisted like a terrible song you accidentally hear and can't get it out of your head, replaying over and over again. I didn't know why it bothered me so much, which only made me more frustrated.

I walked up to the big wooden door, grabbed its knotted handle and swung it open. My hands were so sweaty they almost slipped. It creaked appropriately as it turned on its hinges and I carefully stepped inside. I stood there for a moment, acclimating myself to the coffee smell and the aroma and aura of the calm and caffeinated environment. I inhaled and exhaled--the familiarity relaxing me, pressing the negative thoughts from my body. I looked around and saw her almost immediately. She sat comfortably at a little wooden table for two in a far corner. She glanced up and our eyes met and I felt a flutter in my stomach.

I walked over, pulled out the chair from the table and sat. "Hey," I said, smiling, and swallowing down my nausea.

"Hey, how's it going?" Eva said, returning my smile. Little brass pinecone earrings dangled from her ears and she wore the same universal NE fall attire as I did: boots, jeans and a vest.

"Oh, pretty good. I love the fall."

"Same! It's my favorite season by far."

"Same!" I said, matching her enthusiasm and sitting back in my seat. There was a brief silence which is common for first dates after just sitting down, when neither people know what to say despite all the questions they prepared or had shuffling in their mind moments before. Seeing that she had not gotten anything yet, I broke the silence awkwardly, "Do you want a coffee?"

I immediately regretted asking such an obvious answer. *Duh, she wants coffee*, I thought. *We're in a coffee shop and it's morning. Like duh.*

"Yes please! I have a ton of homework later so I might as well get started on the caffeine. My AP psych homework is interesting, but that book is very thick."

I laughed, "I know exactly what you mean, I took it last year. Mr.

Wolf didn't care for me—to put it gently." She raised her eyebrow and the beginning of a smile took form across her lips. "I'll tell you all about it once we have coffee. What do you want?" I took her order and soon she and I were settled, minds buzzing, exploring each other's lives.

We started off slowly. We talked about classes, which teachers we preferred, which classes were most interesting. Then once we were relaxed and were comfortably laughing with each other, we started getting into it.

I sipped my coffee as she spoke. She and her father had moved to New York when she was young but she had spent every single summer since, in Indonesia, where the rest of her family lived. When she spoke about the world, she was thoughtful and passionate.

"Winter here is something that's extraordinarily beautiful. It can be difficult though. The lack of sunlight is depressing. But it's a completely different kind of beauty. It's not a Bali beauty. A Bali beauty is loud, full of life and energy, rushing streams and rivers, waterfalls, birds and animals running and rustling, rain falling or pouring. Here, in winter, there's a tranquil silence which is so different from what I grew up with. Have you ever listened to falling snow? It is completely silent. I'm used to green and loud," she laughed, "and seeing everything turn white? I felt like I was in a different world the first time I saw it. I still do sometimes. Even fall, it feels like I'm in a different world. So many colors, the crunchy leaves, the temperature. It's wonderful. I love it."

She spoke more of her time spent in Indonesia: fleeing from tourists, seeking and escaping to other islands. It turns out Indonesia is absolutely massive, made up of thousands of islands, many filled with huge cities, ancient temples and untouched native villages.

She wanted to travel, to see the world, the entire world. She wanted to run with the bulls, she wanted to climb Mt. Everest, she wanted to skydive and deep dive in the ocean.

I was mesmerized. She was absolutely brilliant. The way she

talked and spoke about the world. If you asked me if I fell in love that day, I wouldn't say yes but then again, I don't think I would've said no either.

She went on to tell me about her time in New York, starting high school there after being for the most part raised in Bali, how different it was, how her world was flipped upside down. She told me about parties, about drama--maybe more than she intended to.

I like to think it was the coffee shop, coaxing memories, lulling the mind with the caffeinated air and dim lights, making it seem like the only thing to do was to speak and pour out your truths.

Eva was just so different. When life became too much, when the stress got to her, she fell into the world more, grounded herself in nature, stepped not away from her reality but more into it, simply observed it from a closer vantage point. She was an adventurer, a traveler, a taster, a seer and a finder. She, more than anything, was curious about the hidden beauty in this world and more often than not, she found it. The only hidden beauty I sought was sitting at a small wooden table across from me.

Then it was my turn. She asked me what it was like to grow up in the same place, with the same people my whole life. I told her everything. How everyone seems so boring, except Charlie and Leland, of course. I talked about how Charlie and Leland were two of the smartest kids I have ever known, how Leland was most definitely going to Harvard and Charlie Stanford, and how most of my other friends were all going to Ivy Leagues. I told her about the schools I applied to, how they were decent but not close to Ivies. When she asked why I only applied to schools in New England, I said it was because I liked the seasons--which was true. When she asked why I didn't apply for—how did she put it?—"any reach schools," I told her I didn't see the reason. I would just prefer to apply to schools I know that would actually want me. That I was being realistic. I never really had a school that I particularly wanted to go to more. In fact, school had never been really important to me.

"So, you don't think education is important?" she asked.

"Education is essential," I said. "Learning is essential. Growing your mind is essential. But I just don't think our school system is the right place for everyone. Even college. It all seems too generic. Too business and money and less learning. There's a difference between education and intelligence."

"What about dreaming? Reaching for something?" she asked with genuine curiosity.

"When do we have time to dream with all that happens in high school? We are taught to want what we want. Why do you think Leland wants to go to Harvard Law so badly? She is one of the most amazing people I know and could do really anything with her life. But she wants to be a lawyer. Not that I think that's bad. I just think it's... well what she was taught to think she wants that. Not that I have a better alternative." I chuckled and shrugged. "And then there's Charlie. He wants to be an engineer. He's a little more removed from society than Lee is, but not by much. He wants to create. He, out of all my friends, will do something amazing, I think. Or at least I hope."

Eva thought meaningfully and asked, "How did the three of you become such good friends? You all are wildly different from each other."

I let out a quiet cackle, "Well, that's an interesting story. It involves me being stupid. Per usual..." I took a sip of my coffee. "When we were in middle school, I think it was like the beginning of 6th grade or something, I was fairly new to the area. When I first got here, I really didn't know how to make friends, or even talk to people. Not much has changed since.

"It was recess one day and I was in the far back part of the middle school property, I don't even know what to call it, the middle school backyard? Anyways, behind the playground was a big group of trees, and behind that was a fence that separates the school's property from whatever is behind it. I was a loner at the time and while exploring, I found a bunch of empty beer bottles kinda hidden under some fallen branches right next to the fence. With lack of anything better to do, I started smashing them."

"Wow," Eva laughed, "an angsty little David!"

"Uh huh," I nodded and smiled, "so there I was throwing bottles against the fence when a couple of 8th graders, Scotty Stevens and Noah Jonson found me. They were big and mean and were about to beat the shit out of me when Charlie stumbled upon us. He was playing soccer on the field nearby and was chasing a ball. Well, when he showed up, they pushed me to the ground and punted his ball over the fence. Right when they were about to go after him, a book came flying out of nowhere and hit Scotty in the back of the head. It was a brand-new copy of *Twilight*. I think the first book must have just come out. That's when Lee showed up. She had been reading (surprise, surprise) in the shade when she saw the bigger kids follow me into the patch of trees. Well, one thing led to another and they went after her which made Charlie and I go after them. We all were tumbling around, yelling, trying to figure out how to fight and not get hit by the bigger kids when Mr. Flynn, the gym teacher, found us.

"Thankfully, what he saw was two bigger kids beating up on three smaller kids. He told Scotty and Noah to shut up and questioned us about what was happening. We didn't say anything since we were kinda all scared shittless. When he noticed the broken bottles, he demanded to know who had done it. All three of us didn't say a word, but just pointed at Scotty and Noah. They went kicking and screaming to the principal's office, Mr. Flynn pulling them both by the ears.

"That's how we met and that's how we started being friends, I guess. And unfortunately, that's how Leland got me hooked on the *Twilight* series."

We sat there for three hours talking and laughing. Once we realized what time it was, we gathered ourselves, hugged goodbye and departed. As we walked back into the world, we awkwardly realized we had parked in the same parking garage and continued to make small talk all the way there. I was treated with another hug goodbye.

I reported back to Leland and Charlie, who were thrilled that it went successfully. From there, well the next month or so consisted of movie dates, one bowling date, and many "study sessions" where we pretended to do work but really just wanted an excuse to see one another. I tried to hide my feelings for her but I was never good at poker. It was obvious that I liked her, and she took her time with me, testing my youthful patience. Eventually (thankfully), she started liking me more too.

II

Eva and I had our first kiss on a particularly chilly fall day. We were in my basement and had just watched one of her favorite movies, *10 Things I Hate About You*. I hadn't seen it before but had to admit it was excellent. I was more of an action movie kind of guy myself but after watching that, romance was in the air and I was not complaining. I turned and looked at her. The credit song, *I Want You to Want Me* was playing and Eva turned and looked back at me. We were close to each other, sharing a blanket with only a little space between us. She smiled at me, and as the music played and the lights from the tv danced across her face, she leaned in and kissed me. Her lips were so soft and as we got closer and turned more into each other, I felt her body. It was strong, muscled and gentle. I ran my hand through her hair but didn't realize her hair was braided and accidentally caught one, yanking her head backwards. It wasn't hard but it still interrupted our very first kiss and it was completely embarrassing. Eva only tossed her head back and

46

laughed.

"You are so smooth, Dave." She said smiling and leaned back in for another kiss.

The weather grew colder and colder, and the leaves that colorfully painted the grass all darkened and grew stiff and crackly. In October, we had our final cross-country race of the season, by which I really mean that Eva, Charlie, Leland and the rest of the team had their last race. I, not participating in one race all season, watched from the sidelines and cheered, yelled and screamed as I saw my friends and teammates race by.

We were deep into classes and everyone who applied to their colleges were now in a state of limbo: trying to maintain their grades, and not let senioritis become a detriment to their GPAs. All the seniors were tense, and that stress slowly funneled down and through the school, affecting everyone, as it did every year.

Mrs. Randolph, though pleased with our reports, encouraged us to keep it up. By then, almost every girl in our SLAM group had a crush on Charlie. It mostly annoyed Lee but I thought it was hilarious.

My other classes were difficult, and Charlie helped me when I asked. I began inviting Eva to most of our study sessions, and she and Leland took an immediate liking to each other. Leland, who I was convinced was more machine than human, began helping Eva with college applications, classes, and even her prep for the SATs.

To clarify, Eva and I never actually said we were dating, although most people assumed so. We realized that we were both in weird, transitional periods of our lives, and even though we were hitting it off and we both really liked each other (though I liked her more I think), I knew that starting anything formal would only complicate and possibly ruin what we had.

Halloween was the first time she and I showed up to a public place looking like a couple. We dressed up as Bonnie and Clyde, carrying plastic airsoft guns left over from my childhood days. I wore my dad's old suit and Eva wore a black dress that made my heart beat fast.

Charlie and Leland dressed as police and pretended to try and catch Eva and I all night. We ran around Tommy Hitchcock's house all night laughing and yelling, that is until some asshole who no one really knew made a very not okay cop joke towards Charlie. That idiot didn't know what he got himself into. Lee brought the wrath of god down upon the guy. I swear, by the time she was done with him, the whole party was booing him out the door while simultaneously giving her a standing ovation.

Despite Lee's performance, Charlie was upset by the encounter. As a white kid, I really didn't understand why it hit Charlie so hard, until the walk back to my house.

All he had to do was pull out his phone and show us a list. "All of these people were killed by police. All black. That's why I'm upset. A police officer is the scariest Halloween costume out there. Don't know why I went along with it." His body shook with every word he spoke.

Until that night, I had never really thought about him being one the few of black students in our school. It was the first time I really acknowledged my white privilege. I realized that I had bragged about talking my way out of speeding tickets to Charlie in the past. I wondered what he thought about.

For the rest of the journey back to my house, we walked in silence. I walked next to Eva with Leland and Charlie walking in front. Charlie hadn't said a word since he showed us his phone but let Lee held his hand all the way from Tommy's house, down the bike path and through my neighborhood. She only let it go when we got back to my house.

By the time we got back, my parents were asleep—my mom upstairs in bed and my dad passed out on the couch, TV still blaring, laptop on, glasses almost falling off his face. We were planning on sleeping in the basement and my mom had kindly set it up for us— pillows, blankets, sheets, folded neatly on the couches and floor.

We were sitting in the basement and no one was really speaking. A very rare uncomfortable silence started to form around us.

"Anyone want brownies?" I volunteered, unable to come up with anything else to say. Everyone raised their hands. "Anyone want some whiskey I stole from Greg before he went back to college?" Everyone raised their hands.

I snuck upstairs to my room and retrieved the full flask of whiskey Greg had accidentally left out. I had been saving it for a special occasion.

Soon, we were all taking sips out of the flask, each of us grimacing in turn, and not-so-quietly making brownies. Halfway through, my dad came into the kitchen after "resting his eyes" and told us to make noise downstairs instead of the kitchen. "Make sure your parents know where you are," he told Leland, Charlie and Eva before saying goodnight and walking upstairs. We heard him pause, and then walk back. "And everyone is sleeping separately tonight, is that understood?" A chorus of quiet "Yes sirs" followed him as he turned and headed upstairs.

By the time the flask was gone, we had steaming brownies and each of us stole just a bit of my parent's wine from one of the open jumbo bottles of Kirkland's finest.

In the basement, we all curled up, bellies full of brownies and as much wine as we could bear to drink—the stuff tasted like spoiled grape juice... which I guessed it pretty much was. We turned on *Sleepy Hollow*, and fell asleep—all separately, of course.

***

Lily cleared her throat. "David? Where is the relevance."

David stopped. "Uh, right, sorry. Can I just add one last thing?"

Lily sighed, "Sure, David."

***

Soon, Eva, Charlie and Leland all began their indoor track season and I started my alpine racing pre-season--there wasn't any snow yet so we mostly went on runs and did wall sits.

Almost everyone in our town had ski passes, since we had three large ski mountains all within an hour and a half from us, but we, the alpine team, were a different kind of skiers. We looked down upon those "normal skiers" and despised the "park rats"—the nefarious snowboarders who lurked in the trick park, evilly grinding rails and throwing helpless children off jumps. I even heard that they performed satanic rituals, trying to summon demons to harass the rest of the people on the mountain. Per skiing law, we ski racers loathed them. The park was their territory, the rest of the mountain ours. That is, until you took into account the Nordic ski trails and back-country. Those Nordic monsters..."

***

Lily held up her hand and stopped David from finishing his sentence. "Nefarious snowboarders? Satanic rituals? Nordic monsters?" She was frowning. "David, I need you to take this seriously."

David tried to suppress a smile but couldn't quite manage. "What?" he asked, chuckling a little. "I mean, it is true... we did hate them. And how can we be sure that they aren't doing those things?"

"David."

"Okay, sorry," he said, letting go of his small smile. His face turned serious. He sighed. "I guess talking about the good ole days just...

I don't know. It's kind of nice. And that was really the last time I felt happy. I just wanted to, I don't know, make it last just a little longer."

"Let's try to focus on the task at hand. As much as some of the memories you've shared are interesting, I am still failing to see the relevance."

"Lily, I'm sorry," David said quietly. It was a light rebuke, but David, who was looking at his hands felt it.

"David, it will be okay. You're doing great so far. And I don't blame you for wanting to relive those happy memories. But that's not why you are here. That's not why we're talking."

David nodded and sighed, "Yeah you're right. I guess it's time then." He stood and walked to his small pile of belongings on the bed. He picked up a book and walked back to his chair. Lily gave it a puzzled look.

It was a small black leather book with a thin black cord dangling in between the pages. The most curious thing about it was its cover-- there were drops of red wax, splattered and cemented onto the black leather cover. The splatters looked like blood.

"A journal?" Lily asked and David nodded. Lily looked at it curiously.

David let out a long breath. "Yes. It's time to get on with it. When everything started happening, I was confused, so hopelessly confused, and when I'm confused, or upset with something, I write it down. Or try to at least."

Lily looked at it, more curiosity showing. "So, you kept a record of your thoughts and feelings throughout the rest of your senior year?"

David's grip on the book tightened, his knuckles turning white. "I haven't been able to read it, not yet."

A silence filled the room. A long, deep silence, and David was relieved that Lily let it sit, let it stay.

Finally, David spoke again, "I'm scared of what's inside, of what's hiding in it. I'm scared that I don't even remember writing it." He looked to the window. "But if it's the price of freedom, then I want to read it."

"Memory loss is unfortunately an effect of depression so it makes sense you don't remember," Lily said mostly to her clipboard. Then she looked up. "David, may I make a comment?" David nodded. "You didn't have to include the journal, but you did." She looked at him thoughtfully. "I appreciate that. Reading from that and understanding how you were feeling while you were depressed will let not only me but you understand more about what happened. Not understanding something allows people to develop fears and doubts which can act as catalysts for the problem. It can expedite symptoms and ultimately become much more damaging than it should be.

"With understanding something, there is no need to fear it. Not only that, but it then becomes treatable and manageable. Which is why it's so important you're talking about this; why it's important that you are opening that journal and that you are sorting through your own memories to identify the problem and understand how you ended up here."

"Look at you being the therapist."

"Hey, therapy's great. What you're about to tell me is not only important to you, but it is also valuable to other people, myself included. You're not the only person who has had depression and gone through this, and despite how many people suffer from depression, we still know painfully little about it. So, any information is very useful."

David looked at Lily. When they had first met, he thought of her as the annoying "Psychiatric Resident" who by default got stuck dealing with him. Now, his first impression evaporated. Now, he saw a professional, someone who knew how to help him. Someone he respected.

"That sounds like a bit of an exaggeration, but okay, let's get to it. Maybe we'll be done before lunch," David said.

"Don't worry about finishing before lunch, I already ordered us some food. A couple PB and Js. I thought it best to keep it light."

David's stomach fluttered, making him nauseous, "Good idea. Alright. What next?" He opened the journal and began to skim the first page. "I'll start here, I suppose. The very first day of depression."

David stretched his arms and sat back into his armchair. "That first morning was weird, and not in a good way. I distinctly remember waking up to my mom yelling..."

LOSING MY MIND

I

"DAVID! You're going to be late! AGAIN! If I get another call from Deb from the office saying Mr. Meyers wrote you up AGAIN, I'm not going to be happy!"

It was a cold day in late November, and I didn't want to leave the warm cocoon of my blankets and face the chill air that had taken up residency in my room. As my mom's voice carried up the stairs and into my bedroom, I burrowed deeper into my bed.

Another "DAVID!" rang from downstairs. I poked my head out and looked at the clock next to my bed and cursed. Only 20 minutes before the first period started.

What's the point? Why can't I just lie here?

Another yell from my mom was enough to motivate me to roll out of bed onto the floor. With one final groan, I stood and started to dress, shivering all the while.

My mom was waiting for me in the kitchen. She was simultaneously loading the dishwasher and sending an email from her phone. When I walked in, she placed one more plate on a rack and turned.

54

"I hope you did your homework last night. Also, when is your first alpine race? Your father wants to go. It will give him an excuse to miss a work call and ski. Your sister took the bus instead of waiting for you. You should be happy to know that she is currently on time. Get moving!"

I blinked and nodded dully. "Uh... I'm not sure, probably not for a while."

I started putting on boots, bracing myself for the cold and the unexpected couple inches of snow we had gotten over night.

"Did you do your homework? Also, when..." My mom's voice drifted from me as I became lost in thought.

Homework? Shit. I forgot. Which classes though? What did I even do last night? I didn't have practice... I just got home, put on a movie in bed... and... Did I even eat dinner? I think I just fell asleep. Shit, whatever. We'll just go over it in class. I don't care.

I was brought back to reality by my mom's voice, "David? David, are you listening to me? What has gotten into you? Are you okay?" For the first time that morning, instead of being rushed and agitated, the idea of something being wrong with me slowed her and a thin layer of concern washed over her. "David, are you okay?" she repeated. "You didn't come down for dinner last night. I knocked on your door but it sounded like you were asleep."

"You mind if I just take a sick day?" I asked unexpectedly, surprising even myself. "Now that you mention it, I'm really not feeling well. And I didn't do my homework. When I got home last night, I think yeah, I just fell right to sleep. Maybe I have a cold or something."

She looked at me suspiciously, "David, you need to be more responsible. School is your number one priority." But then she gave me a long thoughtful look, walked over, and felt my forehead with the back of her hand. "You do feel a little warm. Hmm... I don't know if this is a fever or maybe senioritis is finally hitting you, but either way, you don't look well. You went right to bed last night? Go take a lie down and take a nap. I'll call Deb. When you wake up, do your homework."

I was a little shocked. This had never happened--ever. I've tried to get out of going to school before and my mom usually threw something at me and kicked me in the butt as she pushed me out the door.

She kissed her hand and pressed it against my forehead, smiling thoughtfully at me. Then she turned towards her cell phone on the kitchen table. I began to unstring my boots and place them back on the shoe rack in our mudroom.

"I'm doing this because you have been staying out of trouble recently, something I appreciate," my mom said from over her shoulder. "Maybe it has to do with your new friend, Eva. You two have been hanging out a lot lately. Are you still just friends?"

Maybe I do look bad, I thought. *Still gotta play it cool.* "Thanks mom," I said, "I'll catch up on homework today. But more sleep does sound nice right now."

I began walking back through the kitchen, the warmth of my bed's blankets encouraging my every step.

"Fine, you don't have to tell me about her! I'm only your mother, the person who gave birth to you and raised you!" I smiled but didn't respond. I heard the sound of keys clattering and the sliding sound of bags being dragged off the kitchen table. "If you need anything, I'll be out. So just text me. Otherwise, I hope you feel better. Drink lots of water! Plan on going to school tomorrow!" she called and I heard the front door swing shut.

"Thanks, and yes, yes," I mumbled and meandered my way back upstairs to my room, falling into my bed. I rolled and wrestled with the covers for a minute until they were wrapped around me once more. I closed my eyes and fell asleep almost immediately.

Now, I have never been good at waking up to begin with, but this was different. When I woke up for the second time that morning, I almost couldn't get up. I had an overwhelming feeling of dread and a wanting to stay in my room under my covers for an eternity. I stretched my arms and legs and let out a long and loud groan.

I spent another hour in bed that morning just lying there, not even thinking, just lying there like a robot in hibernation mode. And then, making the mistake of checking my phone, I scrolled through mindless social media until I noticed that another hour had gone by. Two hours I had spent in bed that morning, and it all felt like it could have been twenty minutes. Finally, an urgent need to pee got me out of bed.

While in the bathroom, I looked at the shower. Typically, I loved to shower, loved to feel clean under the scalding hot water. Today, it felt like too much effort. Getting undressed, stepping into the shower, standing there, drying off after and then if it wasn't already enough work already, you even had to get dressed afterwards too. It seemed like a lot, way too much work.

I went back and laid on his bed. I wanted to melt into it. But then a thought occurred to me.

I'm Ferris Bueller and this is my day off!

It was the rallying call I needed and was enough to get me into the shower. Once I was there, it didn't feel so hard anymore. I let the hot water take me away like it always did.

By the time I got the ball rolling and was up for some breakfast and homework, it was almost noon.

I went to the kitchen, drinking coffee and eating eggs with toast while listening idly to my dad's conference call. "The California client expected the Nanos to be in last week. If there are any bugs or if they aren't compatible with their software then we are behind schedule and the Fab needs to stop..."

I was finishing up my meal when he opened his office door and stepped into the kitchen, coffee cup in hand and glasses resting on top of his head.

"Hey Dave, how are you feeling? Mom said that you're sick?" He walked over to the coffee pot and refilled his cup, he looked at me, "Want a cup?"

"Please." I said, handing him my mug. "And yeah, I don't know. I'm just exhausted. Zero motivation to do anything. Last night when I got home, I fell right asleep. Must've not been sleeping enough lately or something. I didn't get a chance to do my homework either."

"Well I hope it's not senioritis that's dragging you down," my dad said jokingly and placed my steaming cup of coffee in front of me.

I nodded thanks to him, "Who knows. How's work?"

"It's good. We think there might be a problem with an order we're about to ship out to a client. There's always a problem," he said, sighing and taking a gulp of his coffee. "Well, so it goes. Hey, could you shovel the driveway today? If you're up for it. I think it's done snowing for now. Didn't expect it to come this early, but I want to stay ahead of it just in case so your mother can get in and out easily. I'm always worried about her slipping."

I sighed. "Yeah, I guess."

"Alright, I'm off, have another call. Let me know if you want to use the snowblower, I can help you get it started. Put oil in before you use it. Also, the gas tank is right behind the rototiller. Back right corner, you know where it is." He started walking but then paused, remembering something. "Oh, David. Make sure to pump the primer

WHERE IS MY MIND?

bulb. I usually do it seven times."

And with that, he disappeared back into his office with his cup of coffee.

I took my cup back to my room and sat at my desk. Using the rush of caffeine, I started my homework. I got through some of it but soon felt exhausted again.

Hearing my phone vibrate, I stood up and laid back in bed. Eva had texted me and I felt a rush of warmness.

Then I remembered her frown, the first time we met eyes. My smile was slowly replaced with a frown of my own. It was haunting. My mind began to wander and I thought about her more, how amazing she was, how adventurous, how smart she was. Though these were good things, as I listed them off in my head, they didn't feel like it. They felt bad. Suddenly, her cute poetry hobby disgusted me, her ability to surf and breeze through tests annoyed me instead of amazed me like they usually did.

Why does she want me?

There was an interesting thought, something that never really occurred to me. Or I supposed a more accurate question would be, *Why does she like me?* I chewed on the question for a little while. I was tempted to draw out a pros vs cons list but decided against it, it felt like too much work. So instead I thought about myself, and how I really wasn't that great. From being a chubby Italian boy, to not being very smart, to not being the best at sports (although I did kill it in a school wide quidditch tournament last year), to not really having any passions in my life.

A side by side comparison showed me how skewed that balance of this equation was. The math didn't add up. My lame personality wasn't enough to excuse all of the other flaws in my character. She had no reason to like me, she shouldn't even have talked to me in the first place. She was a wonder to the world, and I was just a parasite feeding off of it.

It just didn't make any sense to me. Not only that, but why the hell did Charlie and Leland even associate themselves with me? I was a social flight risk, a wild card. Maybe they kept me around for fun, for sport, because it's always entertaining to laugh at the dumb kid. Right? They were too smart for me, I realized then. They and Eva were so far out of my league that it was suspicious.

Why do they even like me?

There was that question again, like a bright irritating light flashing at random. How could one single thought, some simple question rip at the seams of a lifelong best friendship? I figured I was overthinking it and went back to my homework.

I made it ten minutes when my thoughts began to wander. I stood up angrily and shook my head.

"What the hell is happening?" I fumed out loud.

Remembering that my dad asked me to shovel, and seeing as I wasn't being very productive, I decided to take a pause and go do some manual labor.

As I shoveled however, a random and strange hypothetical of what would have happened if I had forgotten to shovel played out in my mind:

INT. UPSTAIRS HOUSE - DAY

Dad storms upstairs angry and upset and hammers on my door-

DAD

David! I told you to shovel hours ago! What have

you been doing? Wasting away the day per usual?

Me

Throws open the door and screams-

The freaken snow isn't going anywhere! I'll get to it when I get to it!

DAD

You'll get to it now! This is my house and you will do what I say!

Me

It's not my fault I live here! You chose to have me! It's your fault I'm so pathetic!

DAD

Spit flies as he shakes his fist in my face-

Well we regret having you! You are GROUNDED! Spoiled! Rotten! Useless!

ME

Probably screaming in agony-

Screw you! Living here sucks! I hate everything!

DAD

No more friends! No more fun! No more anything! You get nothing! Now go! Shovel until there isn't a drop of snow out there! GO!

And so forth, end scene.

That is what I thought about for all of the half an hour it took to shovel. When I was done, I put the shovel away and went inside, stomping my now slushy boots on the mudroom carpet.

"Hey, thanks Dave. Big help," my dad called from his office.

My anger flared, and I was just about to say something when I remembered that the conversation I had was only in my head. He never actually yelled at me... I wasn't actually mad at him... I blinked and remembered further how he asked nicely. Not only that, but my dad would never really say anything like that... I had never even seen him shake a fist... No one really shook their fists when they were mad anyways.

"Uh, yeah, no problem," I called back distractedly.

It was all very confusing. I was exhausted. Everything felt heavy and all I wanted to do was to lie down. So, I drank a glass of water and was gone, retreating upstairs, back towards the *safety* of my room. And for the rest of the day, that's where I stayed.

II

It was late evening when I had finished enough homework to call it for the night. I had ping ponged from my bed and desk for the remainder of the day. It was a sad cycle: I would lay in bed until I found a fragment of energy to do work, would go to my desk and expel that little energy I had, only to fall back into bed feeling drained and weak.

I tried celebrating being done with homework with a movie but my mind wouldn't let me focus. I responded to texts from Leland and Charlie, giving them both vague reasons why I hadn't been in school. I tried typing out how I was feeling in a text to Eva, how confusing today had been and how guilty I had been feeling about having all these thoughts about her and Charlie and Leland. But it ended up not really making any sense and I deleted it.

After some period of time later I surprised myself. I had been just lying in bed, staring at the ceiling, thinking about how I probably wouldn't mind Voldemort killing me with the Avada Kedavra curse, when I got up and walked over to my desk. I sat down and opened the drawer. I pushed some things around, navigating my hand between my graphing calculator, pens, notebooks, a ruler, a little red swiss army knife, until finally I saw what I was looking for. It was a journal, black leather with a black cord to mark the page. I got it a few years back, I thought it was a Christmas present or something from a misguided uncle. Why would I ever keep a journal? Or a better question still, why would my uncle think I needed one? Answers were beyond me.

I opened it. It creaked and cracked as I stretched its spine, telling me that this was the first time it had been opened. Its pages were crisp and smooth.

I picked up a pen and hesitated...

Who really keeps a journal anyway?

I flipped to the first page. I began to write:

This is the Property of

I stopped, unsure of how to proceed.

Who is this by? Me of course... but I don't want it to say it's by me... just in case someone else finds it.

I shut the book and set it on my desk.

I returned to my bed, turned off the lights and laid there, trying to sleep, but unable to. I felt tired, exhausted, but every time I shut my eyes, my mind seemed to refuse sleep, it refused to drift away into the gentle nothingness.

Instead, a snowstorm of memories chilled me to my core. I thought of every time I had messed up at Leland's or Charlie's expense, every time I accidentally hurt them, had lied to them, had been jealous of them. In class, at parties, in middle school. I had always been a burden to them, had always slowed them down. Where were my contributions? What did I give them except anxiety? A cheap laugh? Bad advice?

I put a pin in the thought and moved on. I realized that even in school, even in my classes without Leland and Charlie, I had made mistake after mistake and slowed the rest of my classmates down. My teachers disliked me for being mostly distracting and half the time I misinterpreted the homework and did it wrong. I was dumb, I was an idiot, a fucking joke.

Then it was onto my family. Always being jealous of Greg since he did everything better. My mom's face when she would look from Greg's report card to mine, going from overwhelming pride, to somber disappointment. I relived fights with my parents, fights with my siblings and more, so much more.

Memory after memory snowed down upon me, blanketing me with frozen terror and guilt. In the early hours of the morning, sleep finally came, but instead of an escape, I fell into a prison of twisted dreams that were filled with anger, fear and regret.

I woke up in sweaty sheets, exhausted and upset. My room was pitched black aside from the faint light from my desk clock which read 4:36AM. I laid there, staring at the red neon numbers until it changed to 4:43. I stood, went to my desk, yawned, turned the lamp on and pulled out the journal. I skipped to the second page and began writing.

Dear whoever,

I am confused. Today feels like the longest day of my life and nothing even happened. Or yesterday now I guess. I have all these thoughts and emotions running through my mind and I don't know where they are coming from. Or why I am remembering them. Vividly reliving them. And then there's Eva. I hope she doesn't ever see me as I am seeing myself now. She would duuuump me in a second. Well we're not even dating so she wouldn't even have to dump me. I like her a lot. I like kissing her. I think she scares me, since she's so far out of my league. Frankly, all my friends are out of my league. Friend league. Whatever. Like if our friendship was a group project, I would be the kid who didn't help at all and barely showed up to meetings. That's what they're working with. They deserve better. I just need to get out of my head and focus on not ruining things. Easy. Hopefully I'll never do this again--journaling I mean.

DG

III

In the following days and even the following weeks, the confusion of that day had shaken me. I had not had another mood swing like that since but the blurred memory of it haunted my every footstep, my shadow following me everywhere I went. But, it was easy to ignore, it was just a shadow, and with a well-lit room, it would vanish, out of sight and out of mind. But it always showed back up eventually. Every time the thought crossed my mind I blamed it on stress, since midterms were coming up and Charlie and Leland and the rest of the early decisioners would hear back from their colleges in the relatively near future.

As Midterms fast approached, something strange happened. Both Charlie and Leland vanished, or at least that's what it felt like. They started to prefer studying alone, they had little interest in movie nights or cold morning runs or really anything. They just wanted to study and focus on college in peace.

Trying not to take offense, Eva and I decided to make the most of the situation and spent the days outside of school cozying up to one another. The more I spent with her, the more hopelessly infatuated I became. She finally let me read more of her poetry--most were romantic fall and winter haikus, and as per our deal, I showed her all of my favorite books that I had been reading since childhood. I'd been holding out since they were all mostly embarrassing but she, despite midterms looming, insisted on reading a few. Sometimes we would even read out loud to each other. She was far better at it than me, surprising me with some pretty decent voices. Oh! And we definitely kissed more--which was awesome.

All the while, however, the stress was getting to me. I loved spending time with Eva, but midterms darkened the sky and were about to unleash its week-long terror upon us. In its wake was my own college future. False dialogues with friends became more frequent, and nasty thoughts about seeing my best friends fail tore me apart with guilt. The weight of it all was getting heavy and I was getting tired of carrying it. Even Eva wasn't safe from me.

It happened in the heart of midterms, when papers and exams were pouring heavily down upon us. Eva and I had been studying adown in my parent's basement and papers, highlighted notes and textbooks seemed to cover everything around us--both couches, the coffee table and even the carpet beneath. I sat on the floor while Eva sat sprawled on the couch, laptop resting precariously on her legs with her feet up on the table across from me.

She had just announced that she was taking a "damn study break" and started doing her favorite study break activity: planning for the future. She was so confident when she spoke about it too. She was excited for it and was ready to embrace it--chase it if she had to. I, on the other hand was terrified. My future was so uncertain that planning more than a week in advance was tricky--definitely not advisable.

Usually, it didn't faze me, I was happy for her and would openly contribute to whatever hypothetical she was on at the time. Not that night. I had been stuck on a practice exam for my German midterm and was looking through the textbook searching for an answer--it was a dense language and I was annoyed. Not only that but ever since I had that weird day... well it was hard to explain. It was as if there was a haze forming around my life and everything seemed just a little dimmer. It was barely noticeable at first, but now I could feel it. Small things felt like big things, I was having trouble sleeping more often than not and I was growing increasingly irritable.

"Maybe I should just apply to universities in Europe," Eva speculated. "I know I won't even apply anywhere until next year but still. It's ridiculously cheap at—compared to here, and it would be cool to travel around over there. I could learn French and go to Paris. I've always wanted a taste. Maybe I should ditch Spanish and take French one my senior year," she chuckled to herself.

"Classic," I absentmindedly bristled and turned the page of my textbook.

"What?" She asked, looking up from her screen. When I didn't respond, she asked again, "What did you say, David?"

When I looked up at her I could see anger flicker softly behind her black coffee eyes but she looked more confused than anything. Something inside of me rejoiced and relished this reaction. I was fed up with hearing about all the cool shit she was going to do when she was done with me and I was out of her life. Why wait? Might as well rip the band aid off before it gets wet and falls off anyways.

I wanted to fight with her and I didn't know why. I had wanted to for the past couple days or it seemed so now. I felt tired, gloomy and grumpy--the haze was thickening.

"Well," I said, looking back down, "all I'm saying is that you seem a little obsessed with traveling. It just seems like nowhere is good enough for you."

What the hell did I just say? I thought and was shocked back into focus. I rubbed my face and tried to lamely shrug the comment off.

Eva just stared at me. "What? *What* does that even mean?" She put aside her laptop, took her feet off the table. "Nowhere is good enough for me?" There was steam coming off her eyes, the coffee was getting hot.

Despite my horror of what I had said, I was getting angrier too. A voice in my head encouraged me to press on, to *push her away, rip the band aid off. She's too good for me anyways. End it before she realizes how pathetic I really am.*

I bit my lip in frustration but there was momentum now. "It just seems like you think you're better than us, better than me, like yeah, nowhere is good enough for you," My mind was in chaos. I was battling with myself for control—since it was my own voice countering and contradicting itself over and over and over again. *Cut her away. I need to shut up. Push her away. I need to apologize right now. Cut her out of my life. I want to be with her. I don't deserve her. I think I might love her. I'm pathetic.* I wanted to scream but I instead looked down and stared at my German book, trying to focus on something else, anything else.

There was a heavy silence and I could feel her staring at me.

"Look at me, David," Eva said firmly. It took effort, but I looked up. Concern and anger fought and distorted her face. When we locked eyes, she took a deep breath and let it out slowly.

"To be clear, you're the one who is leaving first, not me. So that can't actually be why you're upset. Talk to me, David. Tell me what's wrong," she said softly. Her eyes were back to their natural coffee brown color but there was a thin gloss over them, making them shine in the basement light.

I wanted to, to touch her, to tell her about these terrible thoughts in my head. So badly I wanted that. But then the pressing weight in my head was back. The wicked voice in my mind was back, whispering to me, commanding me to ruin this, ruin everything, convincing me that the people closest to me deserved better and needed to be removed for their own good. The thought of speaking to her, touching her, vanished--all I wanted to do was to push her away and the easiest way to do that was to make her hate me.

"I just feel like I'm a fascination to you," I blurted. "That I'm just some little learning experience along the way that you'll laugh about with the new friends you're going to make wherever the hell you go next." She stood and made a move to come closer. "Don't touch me," I practically snarled, like some rabid animal baring its teeth. She flinched at my words. "How can you even like someone like me? I'm fucking pathetic. I can't even blame you when you do laugh at me. I guess I'm just waiting for you to get bored of me and move on. To the next adventure, the next fucking experience."

I had no idea what I was saying, words and thoughts just came blurting out and tears threatened to erupt from my eyes. Anger and self-loathing flared and reddened my cheeks and I felt lightheaded.

Her once angry eyes were now filled with pain and shock.

"David," Eva said softly, "How could you ever think that? I have never once thought any of those things. I would never laugh at you. I won't get bored of you." She stood, walked around the table and sat down on the floor next to me. "I would never." She whispered, placing her hand gently on my shoulder. "Is this okay?"

I tensed, but at her touch the storm inside of me subsided and I was left feeling empty and deflated. I burst into tears. I hated myself for what I said and not being able to stop myself.

"I don't know why I said that," I managed to choke out, shaking my head and looking at my lap. Tears burned down my face. "I don't think any of that stuff, I don't even know where it came from."

Eva reached out and gently wiped a tear before it could fall off my chin. This only made me begin crying more. Her kindness, her compassion, her understanding, her willingness to hear my words for what they really were, her ability to simply see through them. I turned to her and looked deeply into those chocolate eyes. "I'm so sorry," I managed to choke out.

"David," she said, wrapping me into a hug, "I know you are stressed--about school, about Lee and Charlie, about everything, but don't let it build up like that. I know you didn't mean what you said, but those words hurt. Even words you don't mean can hurt." She released me from the hug and took a deep breath, wiping away a tear of her own, "I'm stressed too, and it can go to my head too, but please, David, don't take it out on me. It's not fair."

We took a nice long break from studying after that since neither of us could focus. After I promised to communicate with her better in the future, we curled up on one of the couches and put on a movie. After it was over, she packed up her things and kissed me good night.

As soon as she left, I started crying again. I was embarrassed and horrified and angry at myself.

Why am I trying to ruin everything?

Fortunately, midterms proved to be an excellent distraction, an all-attention-consuming emergency. Tests, papers and projects came one after the other after the other. And then, in a whirlwind of last-minute studying and typing, it was over and December break had begun.

I saw and talked to Leland and Charlie since we did share some classes, but even when vacation hit, they were still weirdly distant.

While I was giving Eva just a tiny bit of space due to my

embarrassing behavior, Greg came home from college. We caught up on everything. I told him about Eva and about midterms, told him about getting my college apps ready and my upcoming alpine season. In return, he told me about his college experiences and adventures; classes with professors who actually know what they're talking about, parties, pledging a fraternity, meeting his best friends. It all sounded like a dream, some fantasy world--an escape.

An escape. College was an escape from this.

My mind raced and serious thoughts about college and what it would actually be for me set in. It was a way out of my life now. I only needed to make it to the end of the year and I was free.

This newfound excitement was double edged—as I soon found out. Behind all the enthusiasm and sudden anticipation for something so new and fun were grim realizations.

I'll have to leave Eva, I have to leave Lee and Charlie. I'll have to leave all of them.

These were the thoughts that plagued me, swept through my mind as I tried to sleep that night and for the nights to follow.

I'll have to cut them loose; it will hurt less that way.

On one of my sleepless nights, I opened my journal.

Dear whoever,

Greg's back. He told me all about his adventures in college. It's his second year, and I guess he told me all about college last year, but this was the first time I actually listened to him. What a different world. I want it. It's freedom, that's what it really is. Freedom from this sad person I'm becoming. I can be anyone at college, I don't have to be me… And when I leave, I won't have to face my friends. The distance

71

alone will be enough to cut them away. And when they go to college and meet people worthy of their love, they will forget me. In 10 years, I'm sure they wouldn't even recognize my name. They will be happy that I'm no longer in their lives.

    DG

THE NEW YEAR

I

It was just after Christmas when Leland and Charlie emerged from the caves they'd been hiding in. When Eva and I finally saw them, they offered the expected excuse: midterms and nerves about hearing back from college. It wasn't the heartfelt explanation I'd been hoping for but just like that, like a flip of a switch, I had them back. For the days leading up to New Year's Eve, we lounged about doing a whole lot of nothing, since we were all done with our holiday homework--I lied about doing mine. We played Michael Bublé's Christmas album (despite it being past Christmas), and sang and drank warm alcoholic drinks. Eva's favorite was peppermint schnapps with hot chocolate, and Charlie's go-to was wine but only paired with brownies. We all knew he just wanted to eat the brownies and to look sophisticated drinking wine and all laughed as he grimaced with each swallow of the crimson liquid—Leland especially, smiling and rolling her eyes at his stubbornness. We talked excitedly about resolutions and about the party we were going to go to.

The next night, we congregated at my house. Eva was the first to get there. Waves of twilight hair cascaded past her shoulders and bright silver earrings revealed themselves every time she turned her head. Between her freckled face and the black top that showed off her

73

shoulders, I was stunned. She was beautiful. From her blue jeans she pulled out her phone and took a picture of me.

I laughed and swatted at her. I was wearing a black button-down with the sleeves rolled up and some gray dress pants. I didn't dress up very often and apparently it was worth capturing.

Next came Lee and Charlie, both having come together. Charlie was wearing his classic white button-down shirt (perfectly ironed) and jeans. Leland, on the other hand, was taking somewhat of a different approach.

When she walked through the door following Charlie, both Eva and I's mouths dropped open. She wore a red skirt, heels and a silver top that showed off her trim build. Before I could say anything, Eva practically screamed, "Daamn girl. Just damn. You're freaking hot!" And she ran over to her and made her do a twirl. "You're wearing heels!"

"Well," Leland said, giving a shy smile, "New Year's only happens once a year, right?"

I looked at Charlie. He was looking at Leland with a look I had never seen before. I couldn't quite tell what it was but when he noticed me looking at him, he blinked and it was gone.

We all were standing around the kitchen table when my dad walked in. "Hey kids! Fun plans tonight?"

"Hi, Mr. Garraway," Charlie, Leland and Eva all said in chorus.

"Big party tonight, father," I responded with an airy smile.

He surveyed us, looking over his reading glasses. "Will you be home later?"

"Not if we party properly," I said, my smile widening.

His gaze landed on me. "Be safe. No drinking and driving. Make good choices and look out for each other." Everyone nodded. "Tell you mom goodbye before you go please."

"I need my bag anyways. Be right back."

I jogged out of the kitchen and headed upstairs. I grabbed my backpack which held a foul looking handle of vodka and gave my parent's bedroom a knock.

"Come in." I heard my mom say and I entered. She was laying on their bed, her back propped up with pillows against the bed's backboard and had her laptop sitting comfortably in her lap. She was presumably working.

"Hey mom, we're all heading out. Just wanted to let you know."

She gave me a look up and down. "Where are you going again, honey?"

I sighed. "Mike Glundy's house, mom. Don't worry, we'll be safe and careful and all that other stuff. Dad already gave us the speech."

She gave me a knowing look. "Be safe. No drinking and driving. If you drink, stay there or uber home. I can drive you in the morning to get whoever's car if need be. Make good decisions. And did I already say be safe?"

"Yes, yes," I smiled. "Shouldn't you be getting ready? Aren't you and dad going somewhere tonight?"

"Just sending some last-minute emails and I'm calling it for the night. But don't turn this around on me, young man. I am old, which means I can have legal fun tonight. You cannot. You are not 21. Please keep that in mind and be safe."

I rolled my eyes dramatically, "Yeesss, mom. I love you, but I really have to go." And with that I turned left.

"I love you, honey!" she called after me. "Text me if there's trouble!"

When I got back into the kitchen, Eva and Leland were sitting at the table chatting quietly while Charlie and my dad were talking about something related to engineering.

"Alright," I said, clapping my hands together, "shall we?"

Soon, Charlie was driving us to Mike's house. We didn't take my car since Leland complained about its lack of insulation and general coldness in the winter. Which was fair. We didn't know Mike very well-- none of us had ever hung out with him outside of large parties and probably wouldn't have gone if he hadn't invited the whole cross-country team. But either way, his parents weren't there and we were ready to party our faces off.

Mike's house was pretty big and when we got there, around 20 people were already there. Some played beer pong in the dining room, a bunch of people sat in the living room, drinking, chatting and watching the TV. From the smell of it, another party for the pot smokers was in the basement.

We began mingling with friends and the general crowd. We laughed, we drank and all eagerly waited for the ball drop which was still hours away. I gave Eva some breathing room (no one likes a clingy... friend(?) while at a party) and I entertained myself with some fellow classmates.

After a while of drinking and talking, time started to slip away, and before we knew it, midnight was closing in. An hour before the ball-drop, I felt a hand on my shoulder and turned. It was Charlie.

"Hey, can I talk to you for a second?" he asked quietly. The strangeness of this threw me off and I nodded, knowing something was wrong. He led me through the fray of near drunk high schoolers, pulled me into the bathroom and locked the door.

"You okay? Is everything alright?" I asked, slightly panicked by his unusual behavior.

"It's Lee. I need to talk to you about Leland."

"What?" I asked, suddenly concerned. "Is she okay?"

"What? Yes, of course she's okay."

"Are you drunk?" I asked, narrowing my eyes, confused by his odd behavior. "I don't understand what is happening."

"I've been drinking, but I'm not drunk. I just, can you just shut up and let me talk for a second? Will you do that?"

I took a big gulp from my cup as a response.

"Thank you," he said. "Okay, how do I say this? Leland. She is… We all have been best friends for such a long time. She barely has dated anyone." He paused.

"I know she slept with Adam Stein last year just to lose her virginity since apparently it was a distraction to her…" I said, then put a hand over my mouth, realizing I wasn't supposed to be talking. Charlie didn't seem to notice or he was so used to me not shutting up he didn't care.

"Right? But she hasn't really seen anyone. Ya know?" I remained silent and nodded. "Well, lately, she and I… I don't know. She is the smartest person I know. She's smarter than me. And she's a great runner. And I think…" He hesitated. I raised my eyebrows, waiting for him to go on. He tensed and blurted out, "I think that I really like her."

His voice was low but terribly earnest, almost pained and it took me a moment to digest his words.

I blinked, then let loose a great big toothy grin. "Holy shit, Charlie. I thought something was wrong!" I let out a cackle and clapped him on the back. "I thought she had like died or something. But you just like her? That's the best news I've heard all year." I saw the panic leave his eyes and tension deflate through his body, as if he had finally caught his breath for the first time that night. "I mean that's brilliant!" I nearly shouted. I began speaking quickly as my excitement got the better of me. "Does she know? Honestly, I thought the two of you were meant for each other but I never thought either one of you saw it. You're a total catch and you haven't gone for anyone in a year or so... You're sexy and you can sing. Every girl would kill to have a piece of you. Really, I did think you were gay and was fully prepared to support you. I hear Danny... what's his last name... well a Danny in our school, vague I know, is bi I think and I was thinking about trying to set that up. But here, you were just biding your time and going after the biggest catch in our school. Our very own Leland." When I noticed him glaring at me I covered my mouth with my hand.

"I hate you," he said then smiled, "Do you really think so? I can't tell if she likes me back." His smile vanished and tension came back into his voice. "What if I try kissing her and she gets freaked out? I could ruin our friendship! She and I already have plans of visiting each other next year. I could ruin everything! I could ruin it all. Over a crush. Well it's not just a crush. She's Lee. I honestly don't think she likes me like that. If she did, we would be married by now or something. You know how she is."

"True," I said, seeing what he meant. "Well, I think there is something there. Also, she is definitely dressed to impress someone tonight. It could very well be for herself but it could definitely be for you. Maybe." I cleared my throat awkwardly but continued, "And, if you don't kiss her tonight you will regret it for the rest of your life, not to be dramatic. Well, yes, to be dramatic." I looked at him. "Okay, what do we know about Lee?"

Charlie hesitated, forgetting his nerves his mind mulled my question over. "In respect to what?"

"She likes boldness. But, underneath, she is a gentle little butterfly. Maybe. Well now that I think about it butterfly might not be the best comparison. She's more like a lion. Be bold and be honest. Logic also makes sense to her, so use logic and if she denies you and you find yourself fending for your life well at least you tried. How long have we been in here? People might start getting the wrong idea about us." I smirked at him and sipped my drink.

"Damn it, David, that doesn't make any sense! None of that makes any sense!" He threw up his hands in frustration.

"Charlie, you got this. Let's make a deal, if you don't kiss her tonight, then I'm kissing you. Deal?" I slapped his opened hand before he could respond. "Slap confirmed. That's a deal. Now get out, I actually need to pee."

"Wait! Damn it, David. You're no help. No help at all!"

I opened the door, pushed him out and locked the door behind him. I let out a long breath and looked at the half empty cup in my hand. I put the lid down on the toilet and sat. I suddenly felt exhausted, I wanted to be in bed, under my covers, alone in my room. An overwhelming urge to cry hit me and I stood back up in frustration.

I went to the mirror over the sink and looked at myself. My curly hair was already messy, I looked unbelievably bloated and when I looked into my own eyes I flinched. The familiar hazel, almost green eyes I saw weren't mine. They were the eyes of a sad, broken soul. I was repulsed by what I saw, the creature, nay, the monster that stood there in the bathroom with me. But I was alone.

I could hear people yelling and gleefully shrieking through the door and wondered why I couldn't have fun like a normal person?

Why can't I just be happy?

"Stop being a little piece of shit and start having fun!" I demanded of my reflection, shaking my finger at it accusingly. "Get out of your dumb head and go have fun." I jumped up and down a couple times, even throwing in some shadow boxing jabs. It was a sad attempt to get myself hyped, but it was enough to get me out of the bathroom and back to the party.

II

I walked through the throng of people and spotted Charlie. He was talking to Leland and Eva. I paused, taking in the three of them, unsure of whether or not he had made a move yet. I found myself nervous for him. The more I thought about it, the more I realized how risky it was. The three of us had been best friends forever. What would happen if it didn't go well? Having awkward sexual tension in front of our group of freshmen would not be good... I gauged them, and it looked like all was well. Charlie was smiling and arguing with Leland about something, Eva and a couple other people stood by and were laughing.

Perhaps my little speech worked after all. Not my best, but you can't argue with results.

Eva turned and smiled at me as I walked up. "What are you people yelling about?" I said, joining in.

Leland rolled her eyes, "What constitutes a sandwich. Charlie has fallen into the fallacy of assuming intention is what constitutes a sandwich which clearly neglects food culture and their origins."

I barked a laugh and chanced a look at Charlie, raising a questioning eyebrow. His face remained neutral as he nodded slightly. He was going to do it. I unsuccessfully kept my face neutral and grinned.

Leland noticed the exchange and was quick as lightning with her accusations. "And what was that? Planning? Consorting? Colluding?

Explain yourselves!"

I laughed, "Oh Lee, calm down, Charlie knows you're right, per usual. Fill up your cup and let's have some fun! Why don't we reserve the beer pong table? One game before the ball drop? Eva and I versus you two. What do you say?" I looked at Eva, who smiled in agreement. Leland narrowed her eyes but agreed to go along.

We played with water, taking sips from our personal cups every time Leland or Charlie made a shot. Eva and I were definitely getting a little drunk and were more focused on sarcastically and dramatically celebrating missed shots. Lots of chest bumps were involved and much to our indifference, we lost.

In a victory celebration, Leland and Charlie embraced in a hug. It lasted… longer than the usual hugs they gave each other, and when they noticed this for themselves, they drew apart a little awkwardly. Thankfully, there was a shout that took everyone's attention away.

"Ten minutes!" Mike yelled.

We all rushed over to the large living room area where a big TV showing Time Square and the spectacular ball suspended up high waited for the final countdown. Charlie seemed too nervous to speak but stayed right by Leland's side. But a curious thing happened as time counted down. Leland also quieted as the ball drop approached and for the first time ever, I thought I saw the same look of nervousness on her face as Charlie's.

"Holy shit," I whispered to Eva. She looked at me and raised an eyebrow. "I think Leland likes Charlie. Charlie told me he is going to kiss her, or at least try to when the ball drops."

Eva stared at me for a moment and then wrapped her arms around my neck. "Thank god," she quietly exhaled into my ear. "Leland has been talking about Charlie all night. She told me that she liked him the other day. She has been freaking out because she doesn't know if he likes her back. I felt like a child these past days. 'Do you think he likes me? Can you ask him?' Blah, blah, blah."

I laughed and kissed the side of her head. "Our very own Charlie and Lee. It's like I've seen this coming but it's still surprising. And I'm kinda terrified."

"Two minutes to go!" Mike yelled again.

On the TV, the two commentators were bundled up from head to toe, microphones pressed eagerly to their mouths as they talked excitedly, preparing our nation for the countdown to the new year. We hit the one-minute mark and everyone in the room hushed down.

I glance over at Lee and Charlie. They had moved away from us a little bit and seemed to be quietly talking to one another. It was an intimate conversation by the look of it, both as serious as can be -their eyes locked with one another's. When the 30-second countdown began, they didn't even notice.

I felt Eva grab my hand and my attention was brought back to her. She was smiling at me. In the dim room, lights from the TV flashed across her face and my tipsy mind swam, soaking her in. She looked like some mythical goddess, colors sparkled off her skin and hair and all I could think was how beautiful she was. I looked at her for what could have been a second or an eternity. Either way it wasn't long enough.

I love you...

As soon as those three words rang in my mind, it all began to fall apart.

The thought of loving her fractured me, because I knew that it would never work, I could never work. She deserved better and she just didn't know it.

"10!" the party screamed and the ball began its descent.

I could feel a pressure in my forehead, could feel guilt and despair submerging me in their depths, ripping into my lungs as I struggled for air.

"9!"

I felt heavy and weightless all at the same time.

"8! 7!"

I stared at the screen to try to anchor myself, but couldn't. In my head I was swept away by a current despair. At the bottom of the ocean I found myself, a single realization swam: I loved her, but I could never let her love me. I was broken, defective, poison. She couldn't see that so it was my responsibility to save her from myself. Save all of the people I loved from myself.

I was drowning.

"3! 2! 1! HAPPY NEW YEARS!" The party erupted into a blissful chaos, and I let the screaming, dancing, hugging, and festivities wash over me. I was there but I wasn't.

Eva threw her arms around my neck and kissed me. Time was moving slowly and I could feel everything--her lips, her kindness, my sadness and the weight of every single person around me.

I pulled back and looked into her eyes. "You are one of the most amazing people I have ever met, Eva. Don't ever forget that."

"You make me happy, David," she whispered. Whatever had fractured inside of me broke further. I could feel cracks splintering out from inside of me could feel tears coming. But before I could shatter, something out of the corner of my eye caught my attention.

I looked over at Charlie and Leland and my eyes went wide. They were locked in an intense kiss--not a genteel kiss like Eva and I shared, no, theirs was passion, fierce desire, as if a dam of emotion had burst apart and there was no stopping the flood.

Eva turned and gasped. I forgot myself, I forgot everything. The sight of them kissing, my two best friends, well it shocked me out of my decent and I let loose a booming laugh. I turned Eva's face towards mine again and kissed her fiercely. I felt her smile dissolve, melting into my lips. Her hand reached up and held my cheek, her fingers splitting to form around my ear. I didn't want to think, I just wanted to be. I wanted that moment to last forever—feeling her pressed against my body, feeling her lips on mine, feeling her body radiate joy, knowing that my two best friends were discovering a love for each other and risking vulnerability to obtain it.

I drew back from Eva and let out a cackle of happy laughter. Then, filled with joy and drunkenness, I nearly tackled the still kissing Charlie and Leland to the ground. They drew back from each other looking a little lost and then looked at me. Taking each by the shoulders, I wrapped them into a big ole bear hug.

"I love you people." I pulled back a little and looked at Charlie. "Thank god I didn't have to kiss you. I think it's time to celebrate? What do you think?"

The both blushing Charlie and Leland erupted in relieved laughter and just shook their heads.

"Let's celebrate! Shots!" Eva half laughed, half yelled and stepped around me to get in on the group hug.

We took shots, we sang, Charlie and Leland kissed more and Eva and I heckled them lovingly all through the night. It would have been a perfect night but dark thoughts lurked in the shadows of my mind, waiting.

We drank into the early hours of the morning. By 4 AM, Mike's living room was a sea of sleeping bodies wrapped and covered in blankets. Mike never made it to his bed, and instead passed out in the bathroom tub holding the hair of a girl named Ashley. She had fallen asleep with one cheek on the toilet seat.

When everyone was asleep, I went outside and sat on Mike's front steps. It was a cold morning, and cold thoughts swirled in my head.

I thought about Eva, and Charlie, and Leland—about everyone. I found myself feeling a deep sadness, a profound inevitability. All my friends, all of my family, all of them--they were all too much. My life felt heavy and hopelessness weighed down upon me. I needed to escape them, to be free from them. They deserved better than me. A tear rolled down my face. Its wake felt like an icy cut in the January cold.

III

Just before the sun rose, Eva found me outside.

"David, is that you?" I could hear her smile. "Hey, are you okay? I've been looking for you." I didn't turn or speak. "What are you doing out here?" she asked gently, sitting down next to me.

My tears had subsided and I stared coldly out towards the slowly glowing sky in the distance.

"I'm just waiting," I said, my voice quiet, trying not to break the fragile serenity of the new morning.

"And how long have you been waiting out here?" She put her arm around me, not feeling the coldness of my body through my coat.

"A while. It's easy to think out here," I said, knowing that the last thing I wanted to do was to keep thinking, to be left alone with my distorted and disgusting thoughts.

"You remember when I told you why I liked the winter? It was our first little date."

"You said you liked it because it was so different from all the noise back in Indonesia. That it was a quiet beauty, something that you've never seen before."

"Yeah, that's it exactly." I heard her smile again. "This place, this quiet, it's all so beautiful. You can hear yourself, hear yourself think. It's like the world paused itself, just for you."

As she spoke, the sun's crown peaked over the distant mountains and started to rise. We sat there in silence, watching the bright orb light up the sky. First purple, then pink, orange and red then finally yellow. How could something so spectacular be so silent, how could it be so quiet?

I thought about Eva's words. How could someone find so much peace inside of themselves? How could they find harmony inside their head? In my head, fear and anger manifested, plagued my mind, whispered to me things that didn't seem right. There was no happiness inside my mind. I was so tired. *I'm not happy. They shouldn't love me; they shouldn't even like me. They should hate me.* I was submitting to that voice, those dark whispers.

I felt Eva lean into me as we watched the cold sun rise. I felt hollow. I didn't feel whole. I wanted to escape.

"You didn't sleep at all, did you?" Eva asked. When I didn't respond, she stood, "Come on, let's get moving and get you home. You can sleep all day, but we do have school tomorrow. Can't have you sleeping in class, can we?" She held out both her hands, waiting for me to grab them so she could pull me up. Reluctantly, I placed my hands in hers. "Your hands are ice cold! Come on then. Let's get you warmed up and get those two love birds up too."

"Eva," I said, without meaning to, letting my cold hands fall out of hers.

She stopped. "Yes?"

"Why do you like me?" I asked.

"What?"

"Why do you like me?" I repeated and looked up into her eyes.

"Why do I like you? What do you mean, why do I like you?" Her voice was playful, until she saw the seriousness on my face, until she perhaps even saw the desperation, the instability and anger behind my eyes. She became earnest, "David, I like you for all sorts of reasons. Why are you asking this?"

My head hurt, a thick wedge of pain between my eyes made my thinking groggy and slow. I could feel anger pooling inside of me. It was an anger at myself, an anger at her, an anger at my friends for loving me, for wanting me. It was selfish of them; it was selfish of me for letting them be fooled into thinking that they should care about me.

"You shouldn't like me. It doesn't make any sense. You're this brilliant person - someone who has seen so much and sees the world for what it is. But for whatever reason, you can't see me." My words seemed to echo, "I shouldn't have come here tonight. I shouldn't have even talked to you in the first place. I should have never become friends with Charlie and Lee. They deserve better, you deserve better. I'm a waste, Eva. I have nothing going for me. I'm just going to be a sad nothing for the rest of my pathetic life." My anger was the only reason I didn't burst into tears right then and there.

The words hung there, suspended between us, colder than the morning air.

She stared at me, blinking, a lost look on her face. Then she recovered. "Where the hell is this coming from, David? You are not pathetic. You're not sad! "We don't keep you around for... I can't even say it, David. Just because I've seen more of the world doesn't mean I'm better than you. That doesn't make any sense. You're a good and nice person, that is why I like you. You are smart. I don't need any other reasons."

I closed my eyes. "I don't even know why Lee and Charlie keep me around. I don't even know why you're talking to me right now. I don't even know why I'm here." I felt my frozen hands clench, creaking and cracking as they balled into fists. "I've been thinking a lot. And I can finally see the truth. I don't deserve any of this. I've wasted away my life. You're only lying to yourself if you think you like me. Charlie and Leland are lying to themselves too. I'm not going anywhere. Nowhere." I shook my head and looked at my feet. "I just don't get it."

"David, stop. I don't know where this is coming from. But stop. We're your friends because we care about you. You have been best friends with Leland and Charlie for forever. Is this because they kissed last night? Just tell me what is going on." She was confused, panicked, I could feel her looking at me--trying to look into me. When I remained silent, she gently repeated herself, "Just tell me what is going on, David."

"It's not because they kissed. I'm happy for them. Now they have each other," I said, breathing out each word. "I just don't get how you could like a person like me."

She responded without hesitation now. "I like you because you are smart, you *are* funny, you make me happy, when you read you squint and make weird faces, and you surround yourself with the best and most genuine people. I care about you, David. But I don't understand what's happening, why are you saying these things? These things you're saying, they're cruel. To me, to Lee and Charlie and to yourself. It is not fair to say or even think that. I know you've been a bit off lately. I've noticed. And I've tried to be respectful and not pry but now I need to know. Please just tell me what's really bothering you. Did something happen? Please, David. Please tell me. Let me in."

"No. Nothing happened. You shouldn't care about me," I muttered and looked to the rising sun. "I don't want you to. It's for the best. I don't think we should see each other. I don't think we should talk anymore. I think you and everyone else should just move on with their fucking lives and just leave me alone."

I was so tired. Exhausted from the party, from sitting out all night, from thinking, from speaking to her. She deserved happiness and all I could offer her was disappointment. Why couldn't she see that?

"Just move the fuck on and leave me alone."

"Who the hell are you to tell me what is best for me?" she practically yelled. "Who are you to tell me what to feel? I don't need a reason to like you, David. I don't know if your drunk still or what, but this conversation is over. We'll talk when you start thinking straight." She turned stiffly away not reaching for me this time. "I'm gonna get Leland and Charlie so we can get the hell out of here."

I sat there and waited - five minutes, ten, and then twenty minutes. Finally, Charlie, Leland and Eva all came out. Charlie was in a dreamy state and Leland looked almost fully functional. She smirked at me and said, "You look terrible."

I didn't laugh or smile. "Let's leave," was all I said. I stood, legs aching from sitting for so long, and turned to walk to the car. Eva kept her distance from me.

"You okay, man?" Charlie asked. There was concern in his voice which made me icier, angrier and when I didn't respond I heard Eva murmur something to them. Talking subsided from there. Eva forcefully took shotgun, I was in back with Leland who kept awkwardly glancing at me. Charlie dropped me off first, per my request, and I left the car without saying a word.

When I got up to my room, I flopped down in my bed. Tears streamed down my face as anger, that anger coming from somewhere I didn't know or understand raged up in me once more, making me even more confused and cry even harder. How could I have hurt her like that? What kind of monster would say those things? Why did I do that? I couldn't stop crying, couldn't stop shaking. I didn't remember falling asleep, only the blackness that swallowed me up.

***

"So that's when you started pushing people away? Isolating yourself?" Lily asked quietly from her chair.

"It is," David said. He wiped a tear away from his cheek. "It's still so frustrating. I didn't mean to say those things. I can hear it now - my voice but not me controlling it, saying those words. But it was me." David unclenched his firsts and saw that there were fingernail marks on both his palms.

"Do you want to take a break?" Lily asked.

David picked up the sandwich that had been quietly delivered as he had been speaking.

"I'll talk and eat."

Lily considered this. "Only if you want to. But, while we're stopped, did anyone besides Eva notice your changing behavior? Did anyone attempt to talk to you about it?"

"After that morning, yes."

THE NEW ME

I

Dear whoever,

I have come to the sad conclusion that I am broken. Broken and beyond repair. I'm sad and tired and mad all the time. And the worst part is that I don't know why. Why can't I just be happy? Why can't I just go back to my normal life. I find myself hating life more and more but I don't know what to do or how to stop it. I feel like I'm burning inside and the smoking is clouding my mind and thoughts. I can't talk to anyone about it. Charlie wouldn't understand. Leland? Forget it. Eva? She wants to understand, but she's better off without me, without this thing that I am becoming. I don't know who I am anymore. I hate it. I hate myself. How do I make things the way they were?

DG

It was more than a week after the New Year's party and I sat in the kitchen, staring at the plate of food before me. It was early. I had come downstairs after waking up from yet another bad dream, giving up on trying to fit in an extra hour or two of sleep before school. I didn't do my homework. Again. I tried to remember what I did last night. I couldn't. Not my homework lol.

I had barely spoken to Leland and Charlie, although I was sure they were too caught up in their little romance to even notice.

I heard footsteps behind me. "Morning, David," my mother said as she walked around the table, smiling. "You're up early. Finishing up some homework or something?"

"Something like that," I mumbled.

She was going through her morning routine of eggs and getting the newspaper from outside when she took a moment to stop and look at me. "David, why are you eating left-overs for breakfast?" When I didn't respond, she came to the table and looked intently at me. "David, what has gotten into you lately? You seem so down all the time. Did you get into a fight with Eva or something? I haven't seen her in a little while. Or Charlie or Leland."

I looked down at the cold pesto pasta from the night before. It looked sad on my plate. It tasted sad. I sighed.

"Everything's fine, mom." I said, my voice monotonous, almost robotic.

"I don't think so," she said, frowning. "I have barely even seen you this week. I know you're busy, but it would be nice to be able to have a conversation with my son once in a while. Stop being stubborn and tell me what's wrong." She smiled, "I am old and wise. I'm sure I can help. Talk to me."

I put my head in my hands and closed my eyes.

Leave me alone, just leave me alone.

"I'm fine." I whispered.

"David…"

I slammed my hands down on the table,"I. Am. Fine!" I yelled. "Holy shit. Just leave me alone for once." I stood up, leaving my food on the table and walked out of the kitchen. All I heard was silence. I walked fast towards the safety of my room.

Once my mother regained her composure, she came right after me. "Excuse me?" she hissed. "What did you just say to me? How dare you shout at me like that!" She caught my arm right as I was turning the corner to go up the stairs. "Grounded. Grounded for the weekend and next week. Do you hear me? And so help me god if you slam that door," she pointed upstairs to the direction of my bedroom door, "it will be two weeks. I don't know what is happening with you but I don't like it."

"Whoop-de-fucking-doo," I snarled.

She stood there open mouthed, not comprehending what was happening. She looked at me like one looks at a crazy person, a lunatic on the street, a stranger. I ripped my arm out of her hand and stormed upstairs.

For the weekend and the entire next week, I cried myself to sleep. I had good days and bad days, but each ended the same: me in my room, alone with the lights off, tears running down my face for reasons I didn't understand. I had no energy anymore—no will or want to see people, to talk, to breathe. I just wanted to disappear, wanted people to forget about me while I slowly embraced a void of nothingness.

II

I skipped out on my freshman "Slammers" (as they were called (unfortunately)) that week since I just didn't see the point anymore.

Randolph had noticed my change in mood - had noticed when instead of participating, laughing and distracting our class like I usually did, I was silent and withdrawn. And later that week, she cornered me after class. It was a Friday, mid-January-ish, and Randolph was just finishing introducing our final community service project—something all of the SLAM leaders would have to plan and coordinate with their own groups.

"So, like I said before, you need to reach out to places within our community, and see what volunteering opportunities they may have or need. If you can't think of any places, I have a list of places previous SLAM groups have gone. With that being said, I would prefer if you came up with the place and idea yourselves. All of you are smart people who care about this community. Now I want to see it." Randolph finished with an encouraging smile right as the bell rang. I got up to leave, not having taken anything out of my backpack, and walked towards the door. "David, could you stay for just a minute? I'd like to have a quick word."

Dread filled me. *What the hell does she want?* I reluctantly turned, navigating through the current of exiting students, carefully avoiding their eyes and slumped back down into my seat. I didn't see Leland or Charlie leave. A few other students stayed to ask questions about the service project and after 10 minutes, Randolph and I were alone in her classroom.

"What's up?" I said, trying to feign enthusiasm and giving her a vanishing smile.

Randolph placed a chair directly in front of me and sat. "David, you missed both of your Slam sessions this week. Leland and Charlie need you there. It's not fair to them if you skip out like that."

"Yeah, I'm really sorry," I said. "I just forgot, I'm pretty behind on my homework, ya know? I didn't really get any work done over break and now I'm stuck playing catch-up."

"David, I'm sure that's true, but I just want to check in on you.

You seem a little off lately. Although missing SLAM is not okay, I'm not mad at you. Leland and Charlie are two very capable people. And all three of us are concerned about you." A wave of heat and annoyance flared through my body. "They came to me and told me that they think something happened?" Anger sparked inside of me. *How dare they go behind my back and talk to Randolph?!* "And that you haven't wanted to talk to either of them for a little while now."

She was right, I had been avoiding them like my life depended on it. In class sitting as far away as possible, skipping SLAM, Charlie even came to my house one night and I turned him away.

She looked at me meaningfully. "It can be hard when friends fight. You might feel like you can't talk to them, and that is a huge outlet being cut off. This is an incredibly stressful time in your life and friends are important. It's not healthy to keep things bottled up inside. You're such an extrovert, David, and I see it in class all the time. You love talking to people, laughing, joking. You brighten this room, even if you can be slightly distracting sometimes. But that's your outlet, David. The people around you."

"I'm fine. Like I said, I'm just behind in work." I said, trying to ignore her words. "I need to go. I have an alpine meeting I need to get to. We have a race tomorrow."

Randolph pursed her lips. "I think you should just talk to them, David. But if you don't feel like you can, I'm here for you. Think of me as a resource. I'm here, David. You need only ask."

I stood. "Thanks for the offer, but I'm fine." Randolph was about to say something in response, but I cut her off with a quick, "Have a great weekend," and fled out of the room, leaving her standing in front of my empty chair.

I was almost halfway down the mostly empty hall when I heard a voice behind me.

"David, don't be mad. We were just worried."

I stopped and turned around, recognizing Charlie's voice. Leland was standing beside him. They had been waiting for me.

I glared at them and turned quickly and walked away. I could hear them following me. "Since you're following me, please don't go behind my back and tell a teacher about my life." I stopped and turned to face them. "Since when can a teacher help? When has that ever worked?" Two students nearby glanced over at us and politely turned away, walking in the other direction.

"Man, come on. We were just trying to help. Eva is freaking out. You haven't talked to her or to us. We miss you," Charlie said.

"And you've been avoiding us," Leland added.

"Then talk to me. Not to freaken Randolph," I spat.

Leland rolled her eyes. "We've been trying. You haven't responded to our messages, you skipped SLAM and you turned Charlie away after he drove over. There's more too. Would you like a list? We had no choice." She crossed her arms in front of her. "What's going on with you? You've been downright cruel to Eva and it's not fair."

"I don't like Eva. Simple as that. You should just leave me alone."

"Bullshit," Leland snapped. "You're in love with her. Is that it? You're in love with her but you're leaving soon? So you don't want to get attached?"

"Oh, fuck off Leland," I said viciously.

"You can still see her when you're at college, David. You can visit. We are..." Leland said, trailing off.

I didn't understand for a moment. Then it clicked. "When did you hear back?"

"Two days ago. Both of us," Charlie said.

"Well, congratulations. Never had any doubts." My words were dry. They looked at me, hurt by the lack of excitement in my voice. I paused again, something occurring to me. "Wait, how are you even going to make that work? Long distance across the entire country?"

There was a pause and they glanced at each other.

"I'm not going to Stanford..." Charlie said.

I blinked. "You applied early decision, of course you are."

Charlie looked uncomfortable and shuffled his feet, "I applied early action. Not early decision. He let out a breath, "I thought I was going to apply early decision but I panicked at the last moment, and changed my application. My parents kept saying it was way too far away... and well..." He looked at Leland.

"You did it for Lee," I said. "So... where are you going? Harvard too?"

Charlie laughed softly, "No, not Harvard. I'm going to Northeastern. It has a great physics and engineering program. My parents are just happy I'm going to be on the east coast. I did get into Stanford though. But I'm choosing Northeastern," he said, glancing at Leland again.

I was about to smile, to congratulate them, but something held me back.

"You didn't hear back two days ago from Stanford or Northeastern, did you?" I asked.

Charlie looked guiltily at his feet, and then back up at me, but before he could respond, Leland cut in. "He found out from

Northeastern a while ago, and Stanford earlier this week. I found out about Harvard two days ago."

"I was going to tell you," Charlie explained. " I wanted to talk to you but you've been avoiding me and I have no idea why."

Realization about his visit struck me and I felt sick with embarrassment and guilt. I swallowed it down.

"So that's why you and Lee were off the grid before break?" I asked.

"Yeah. I mean that's a part of it," he said, shrugging

"You could have come to talk to me."

"Dave, come on. Sometimes you have to figure things out yourself before you can talk to others about it. But you were the first person I wanted to talk about it to."

"Why?" I asked.

"Because you're his best friend, David." Leland answered and I scowled at her.

"Great, well fucking have fun."

"What is that supposed to mean?" Leland said, her voice raising.

"Lee," Charlie said warningly. "David, I asked you because you're my best friend and wanted your help. I'm sorry I didn't tell you sooner. And I did try to come over..."

I chuckled bitterly. "You barely explained yourselves! Both of you. It felt like I didn't have friends for an entire month! 'Midterms' and 'college.' That's all I got. So, nah, no biggie. You're right. You two will do great next year." I turned to go. "Oh," I said, pretending to remember something. "Next time, no need to tell me. Not sure why you even tried to begin with." I walked away.

"Come on, what are you talking about?" Charlie said, hurt in his voice.

"David, what *are* you talking about? What happened? With you? With Eva?" Leland demanded.

"Back to the fucking Eva thing again." I yelled, spinning on them. The last couple students in the hall ran for it. I felt rage inside me now, boiling to the surface. "I don't like her, I'm not in love with her." Words started flying out of me. "I hope you two have a lovely time next year. You're perfect for each other. You really don't need me anymore. The two of you are just smart assholes and honestly I don't know why we were even friends. It's pathetic. You two deserve each other. And as far as Eva goes, I don't give a shit about her. She's just gonna move on to the next fucking adventure!" I couldn't stop. A furry that didn't belong to me took over. I felt the release of the painful pressure I had been holding inside, crushing and pressing against my lungs, my head, my heart. "So why don't you both fuck off. Why doesn't everyone just leave me alone? I'll do everyone a favor and speed up this little process and—"

Charlie stood there open mouthed but Leland cut me off. "David, what the hell is happening? What are you doing? Did we do something to make you think all of those things? Where the hell is this coming from? Eva loves you, David. Are you hearing me? She. Loves. You."

Eva loves me? Her words hit me like a cold slap but I barely felt the sting, my mind was numb with a wintry rage. *Who would love me?*

My insides were screaming, my blood and beating heart urged me to stop this madness, to stop pushing the people I loved the most away. But no.

"Fuck both of you. Stay away from me."

"David!" Leland reached for me but I stepped away.

I looked dead in her eyes and snarled, "You are a manipulating control freak. Afraid of losing me because you can't make any other friends? Sad because you can't make me be your friend? Can't control everything in your life? Fuck off." I fled. Charlie and Lee didn't say anything, didn't call out, didn't even move. They simply stood there, stunned into silence.

My alpine team meeting was no longer important. I just needed to leave. I raced out of the school and was halfway across the senior parking lot when I heard something that made my heart lurch.

"David!" Eva yelled. I could hear her running towards me. "David, stop!" To my surprise, I did. I could see my car, could see an escape from her and her words that were going to hurt me. *Please no. Please just walk away, Eva.* She didn't. "Look at me." She demanded.

I turned and looked at her. She was beautiful, with her brown eyes, her two black braids, her skin, her lips. I could feel tears building up.

"What do you want?" I managed to choke out.

"What do I want?" she asked incredulously, taking a firm step towards me. "I need you to tell me what's happening! I need to know if I did something to hurt you!" I could see tears in her eyes now. "We had such a good time that night. It was perfect." She took a breath. "What happened?" She asked through gritted teeth. "I don't understand."

A car honked at us to move but neither of us paid attention, leaving it to navigate awkwardly around us.

She deserves better. I don't deserve her. I deserve to be alone.

"Eva," I said slowly, "I don't want you in my life."

I could see hurt in her eyes. And then she blinked and pain disappeared. In its place was anger.

WHERE IS MY MIND?

"That's bullshit and you know it!" She yelled. "That is such fucking bullshit, David! Why won't you just let me help you? Stop lying! To me! To yourself!"

"I'm not a charity case! I don't need your fucking help!"

"I never said you were, David!" She said. "Why are you trying to push me away?! Is it because you're leaving?"

"That's not it at all!" Desperation was creeping into my voice.

"Then tell me, David! Just explain what is going on and we can work through it. Please... I don't understand..."

I could feel her, feel all the love and care that she wanted to give me. But I couldn't accept it because if I did, she would get hurt even more. I just wanted her to hold me, to touch me, but my mind wouldn't allow it. I wanted to scream that I loved her, but the words wouldn't come out, couldn't come out. Instead, to both my own horror and pleasure I spoke—not words of love, but words that ensured I never hurt her ever again.

My voice was lifeless, my eyes hollow. "I never loved you," I lied. "I never cared about you. Just stay the fuck away from me."

I saw her eyes gloss over, then tears started trickling down her freckled face. Even when sad, even when crying, she was beautiful.

I left her there, standing in the middle of the parking lot. As soon as I reached my car, I began crying too. I cried and screamed the whole ride home—almost running off the road a few times. When I got home, I snuck past my parents and my sister to my room where I cried myself to sleep once again.

III

The next day I woke up with swollen eyes and a pounding headache. I skipped breakfast and drove to school where I met the rest of the alpine team. They were already loading their gear into the bus when I got there. I hurried to get my gear and skis in with the others. When I turned, my coach was standing there, arms crossed and looking rather displeased.

After I apologized and made up an excuse for missing the meeting the night before, he caught me up on the bus. The state championship was coming up and this race and how well we did would determine our team's seed going into states. Only a select number of racers per team could go so our coach was making a roster, saying wearily that he would have to make some people stay home. Today was a slalom race.

We did some practice runs and I tried to get my head into it. But I couldn't. When it was my turn to race... halfway through I caught an edge in a flush. One of my skis ejected and I was sent flying down the course and slid to a stop near the safety netting that lined the side.

I sat in the snow and stared at my now ski-less ski boot. The realization of my failure seeped through my GS suit along with the bitter cold.

When it was over and we got back to school, Coach held me back and told me that he wasn't bringing me to states.

I spent the rest of the weekend in my room, lights off, only leaving to get food or use the bathroom. What was I doing? Nothing. For hours. All the while I would try not to think. Thinking was toxic and would make me feel worse. Every time I heard my phone buzz with a new text notification I would flinch away, shutting my eyes tighter.

An unwelcomed surprise greeted me when I got to school on Monday during home period—which I showed up for this time. Deb from the office, which is how everyone knew her by, came and retrieved me. It wasn't a SLAM day so although Leland, Charlie and I were all there, we weren't really interacting with our freshmen. Most of them were doing homework while a couple of the boys fooled around in the back of the classroom. I had been staying a careful distance away from Charlie and Leland, not looking or talking to either one. The only reason I was there was because I didn't want Randolph to talk to me again.

When Deb walked into our classroom and asked for me to follow her, I was a little relieved to have an excuse to leave but was not thrilled that someone else wanted me. I drew some stares as I was led out.

I followed her reluctantly down the hall. This attention inspired complete dread, as most things did lately. After walking for a minute in silence, Deb led me to the guidance office. My heart sank.

As we entered the office, we were met by my more-than-useless guidance counselor, Mr. Holden. He wore a smile which (I'm sure) made other students feel comfortable and malleable. His glasses were thin, and so was his hairline. A once chestnut brown head of hair was now graying and retreating back—as if it were dying and trying to escape.

He nodded a thanks to Deb who promptly left. Mr. Holden led me to his office and shut the door behind us. It took my last remaining self-control to stop from flinching at the sound. His small office was decorated in self-motivation posters and pictures of his family. I sat in a plush and heavily cushioned chair that faced his desk. He walked around and sat, looking at me with his stupid smile.

What an asshole.

"David, hello. Thanks for coming to see me today. It sure has been a while -since we met about college last year. Wow the time sure does fly," Mr. Holden said cheerfully.

"Sure," I said back, my voice monotoned.

"I just wanted to check in on you. See how your year is going so far." Mr. Holden said, leaning forward in the chair and putting his elbows on the desk. He waited expectantly for me to say something.

"It's going fine," I eventually said, maintaining my newly mastered robotic speech. No one wants to talk to you when you sound like a dying computer.

Mr. Holden's smile didn't fade. It was annoying.

"David," he started. Just from hearing him say my name I could hear the concealed concern start to show itself, like brown sludge leaking out of a sewer pipe, his voice reeking of complete and utter bullshit. "I've been in touch with a few of your friends and even a few of your teachers. They said you have been a little down in the dumps and I just wanted to check in." He paused and looked expectantly at me. "This is a huge transitional time in your life, you have college on your plate, all your senior classes, and I'm sure senioritis is hitting you hard." He chuckled as if he made a joke. "On top of that you have your freshmen Slammers to look after and all kinds of sports teams you're on, not to mention being social with your friends. That is a lot to handle, David."

I didn't say anything. I knew all this.

Gee thanks for reminding me of all my freaken problems.

When I remained silent, Mr. Holden continued seriously, "We want to make sure you have the help you need to get through this year, David. Some of your teachers admitted that they have seen a declining effort, that most of your homework is incomplete. And I think I know what's going on..." he trailed off and his smile returned. "Senioritis is a very real thing, and I really hate to see you fall victim to it. But I get it! David, I get it. We've all been there. All these pressures are weighing down on you, you just want to leave and get out, you think you need to get done with this year as quickly as possible. David, college is waiting for you, and the most important thing is to cross one bridge at a time. You're on the senior-in-high school bridge right now. Let's cross that one and see where we are, shall we? We're not gonna let some senioritis stop you from crossing your bridges! So, keep that chin up." He finished encouragingly with a chuckle that made my ears want to bleed and a smile that made me nauseous.

"That sounds good."

I left Mr. Holden's office saying only seven words total.

But as I walked down the hall, I understood something: people were noticing. In order to stay under the radar, in order to avoid fun little meetings like that one, or being cornered after class, I needed to get better, or at least pretend better. The problem with that was I was actively getting worse -becoming more and more sad, more and more angry, more and more lost.

***

"What I needed," David said, "was an outlet. Which is exactly what Randolph said. I had lost all of my outlets."

"What were they before?" Lily asked.

"What Randolph said mostly. Friends. Doing stupid things. Getting into trouble. Laughing..." David said, trailing off. "I used to laugh all the time. More like cackle really. In middle school I got the 'best laugh' in my class superlative. It's stupid, I know, but that was me. My loud and annoying laugh would get everyone going, sometimes even the teachers."

"And you found an outlet?" She asked, glancing at his arm.

David noticed, and gave her a sad and tired smile. "I did."

THE OUTLET

I

I was getting worse and I didn't know how to stop it.

The next week I attended both days of SLAM, during which Leland and I openly argued with each other over totally menial things, leaving our homeroom teacher and our Slammers all open mouthed.

I did my homework just because I knew if I didn't, I would be called right back into Mr. Guidance Counselor's office and I would be forced to speak, to be talked down to and humiliated. But the quality of the work was pathetic; I skipped things and left them blank, and the things I actually filled out were usually wrong.

Each night when I got home my mother would try and greet me. I would ignore her, but she was as stubborn and persistent as I was. My rudeness and seemingly unexplained nasty behavior drove her crazy, and we would usually walk away from one another screaming. My dad would always break it up (or try his best to), at a complete loss of what to do and having no idea what we were arguing about to begin with. They were both scared. But that didn't stop my anger from lashing out. I didn't know where it came from. It was my temporary outlet I suppose. It released some of the pressure inside of me, but it wasn't working well enough.

The only place I was not a complete walking mess was my room. My safe place. I would not move, dread leaving, think terrible thoughts about people—all that good stuff. I just wanted to sleep all of the time but I usually couldn't. I would lie awake in bed all day and all night. I would cry all the time, sometimes for no reason and sometimes because I had ruined all my friendships and pushed everyone I loved away. I would cry until my eyes burned and I had no tears left.

When I was out of my sanctuary of sadness, I continued to push people away. I had requested to switch lab groups in my physics class. Mr. Ellis was confused and at first said no, but once I fed him some decent lies, he switched me. I knew changing groups would hurt Leland and Charlie. I didn't want to do it, but I knew if I kept hurting them it would be easier for them to let me go. I couldn't let them love me.

It helped that lies came so easily. It was because I simply didn't care about anything. I was becoming detached from reality. Lying became as easy as breathing, slipping out unintentionally, making up excuses for why I hadn't turned in a paper, why I couldn't hang out, why I looked like I hadn't slept in 10 days.

The mere thought of Eva became a thought-crime, a mental taboo. It caused too much pain to even think of her, so I tried my best to shut her out of my mind completely.

One day as I walked through the halls of the school, trying my best to be invisible, I heard someone say something that caught my attention.

"I could use a drink."

I didn't know who said it but hearing that made me realize something.

I could use a drink.

I was grounded when I texted Mike Glundy. Why was I

grounded? I couldn't tell you, but during those days I almost always was. Why Mike? Because I didn't really know him and he didn't really know me and I knew he was always up to something. So I hit him up and surprise, surprise, a girl named Ashely Carmichael who was having it. She didn't go to our school, but instead a neighboring one. The fact that I was, for the most part, going to be partying with complete strangers was reassuring. I had never hung out with Mike when I wasn't with Lee or Charlie, so I was nervous. I almost backed out several times. Not only that, but...

***

Lily raised her hand and David paused and raised an eyebrow.

"Question?"

Lily nodded her head. "Before we go on, were you ever able to reach out to Mrs. Randolph? She seems like a good person to seek help and support with."

David sighed. "No, asking for help of any kind was really off the table. Anytime anyone showed any sort of support towards me, even kindness, I would just get blindingly angry or just shut down completely. I saw them as a threat I guess."

"One thing depression seems to be good at is isolating people and that can take form in a variety of different ways. Emotional isolation can be just as bad as physical isolation and it sounds like you were doing both. And anger is a common defense mechanism for even people who aren't depressed." She leaned forward and continued passionately, "So often people get angry when offered help because they perceive it as a weakness, when in reality it's our strengths as human beings. We are stronger in number and that means being able to accept help. And that means putting yourself out there and being vulnerable. For whatever reason, the definition of vulnerability has been warped, thought to be meant as being opened to attack or putting yourself in harm's way. I couldn't disagree more. To be vulnerable is to be strong." Lily stopped

and cleared her throat. "Sorry, I'm getting off topic. My senior thesis back in the day had a lot to do with the concept."

"Right," David said slowly, "I mean yeah, sure."

"Enough of me talking, why don't you pick it back up?" Lily chuckled.

II

The night of the party, my parents left to go have dinner at our neighbors and soon after they departed, I departed as well. I was grounded and knew my mother would lose it and try to bring whatever wrath she thought she had down upon me, the problem was I didn't care about her or anything she could do. Consequences bore no weight. She and I would fight the next day and she would probably extend my period of being grounded, but what else was new? A part of me was excited for it. To yell. To feel the pressure release inside of me through anger. To have energy instead of eternal exhaustion.

The party was in the basement and when I got there. It had stiff looking rugs but a couple of comfy looking couches. A few people were playing pong on a plastic folding table but most were lounging on the couches playing a card game. Mike introduced me to the maybe ten people there saying, "This is Garraway, and these," he gestured to the general crowd, "are friends. Now let's get hammered, please and thank you."

For whatever reason, it felt good to be called by my last name. My old friends never did. It also felt good that I didn't really know anyone there and it helped me relax slightly. Being around people still made me nervous and social interactions were something that I dreaded, strangers or not. For at least the beginning of the party, I was awkward and could barely make eye contact with anyone. It helped that most of them were already pretty drunk and incoherent. Mike handed me a drink, invited me to play some drinking games, and as the alcohol set in, I was almost enjoying myself.

At some point, one of the girls there came up to me and introduced herself as Tessa. She was cute, short with dirty blonde hair, light eyes, and a red long-sleeved shirt that complimented her body. I stumbled through the conversation, not really knowing what to say, but she persisted. I had no idea why she started talking to me but soon, as the alcohol dulled my mind and lowered my well-enforced walls, I saw her as a welcomed distraction and even began flirting a little. Soon I was good and drunk but despite my drunken state, I can't forget what happened.

***

David paused and sighed. "I try to forget sometimes, but it's no use. There's no forgetting," he said, shaking his head sadly. "I wish I could go back - never go to that party, never speak to that girl. But I think that if it didn't happen that night, one way or another it would have. It almost felt inevitable. I guess most terrible things are."

***

We played beer pong and kings for a long while. My primary benefactor for drinks most of the night introduced himself as Brandon and he went out of his way to be friendly. With alcohol's help, I was able to laugh and smile without really having to fake it.

When the party started losing steam, Tessa pulled me aside.

"Hey, do you want to go upstairs and talk? Chat for a bit maybe?"

I shrugged, not really comprehending what she was implying but was happy to go along. We took one last shot for the road and she grabbed my hand, the both of us sneaking our way upstairs and from the rest of the party.

The lights swirled and spun in my eyes as her steady pace pulled me up the carpeted stairs after her. I followed like a puppy on a leash, drunkenly bumping into the walls along the way and letting out giggles with each impact. Each time she would shush me and giggle back.

When we reached the upper level, we found ourselves in a brightly lit hallway lined with bedrooms. It became clear to me what she meant by "talk."

She let go of my hand and slowly walked down the hall. When she reached a room, she opened the door and looked back. A playful smile danced on her lips. I stopped at the top of the stairs and stood there dumbly. The thought of Eva flashed through my mind. It annoyed me. I wanted to forget her, and purge her from my memories. And then I was walking to Tessa and away from Eva.

Before I reached her, Tessa disappeared into the darkness of the room, and I followed. She told me to lock the door, and as I did, I felt her fingers begin tracing my body, coming under my shirt. Her nails gently scratched down my skin as her hands slid down my chest, then to my back, finally coming to rest at my waist.

I was frozen in place, feeling her unfamiliar touch on my skin, shivering as her nails traced my back and sides.

It's okay. This is the way. Forget Eva.

Then, before I knew what was happening, I turned and kissed her. It was fierce and angry and sad.

I reached for her body as she began to unbutton my shirt. My hands explored this new terrain--her skin was soft, her body strong but delicate. Although the room was dark, the light under the door from the hallway illuminated us just enough. I pulled her shirt up over her head and threw it behind us. Through my blurring vision I thought I saw a mark on her arm, maybe a tattoo. The thought came and went quickly as more and more clothes started coming off our bodies.

The room was a whirlwind of breathing. We staggered toward the bed, trying to kiss and walk at the same time, performing a funny looking dance with one another. When we hit the edge of it, she pushed me down on top of the covers. I slid my body back onto the pillows and she slowly began to crawl to me.

She reached me, and like two stars in the sky, we collided and I forgot everything. In her embrace I floated through space and time blissfully ignorant of my sad reality. Nothing else mattered. Here, I hid from all the hurt and pain the world caused. I felt weightless.

And then it was over.

"I want to have sex," she said plainly. We were both lying on the bed in various degrees of undress and she gently pulled away from me to speak.

I landed roughly back on earth and though I wasn't surprised, all the momentum we had created left the room with the bluntness of her words.

"I would also like to have sex," I tried to match the tone of her voice, trying to sound casual and to not slur my words. "Do you have a condom?"

"Uh, I don't have one but we don't need one." A seductive smile shone through the dimly lit room and she climbed back on top of me.

I frowned at this. "Of course we do." I said, sitting up on my elbows.

"It'll be fine. Don't worry." She whispered in between kisses and with a hand on my chest, pushed me back down.

My mind spun.

I don't care about Eva, I told myself. *I should be having sex with this girl. The damn girl who is basically naked, on top of me, actively trying to have sex.*

But I couldn't. The prospect of becoming a teen dad shocked the system, overriding it and I took back control.

"Not without a condom," I said gently pushing her away, creating space between us.

She looked confused, and then annoyed. "Oh, come on," she said, "It's fine." She went to push me back down but I grabbed her wrist. She gave a little gasp, glancing at my hand.

"Oh, sorry." I mumbled, letting go.

"Whatever." She was annoyed. She climbed off and laid down next to me on the bed.

As soon as she was off me I was suddenly lost in my drunken and dark mind.

What a mistake it was coming here tonight. I want to leave. I never should have come.

Thoughts of Eva and of how pathetic I was came cascading down upon me and I felt like I was going to puke. I wanted to cry. I wanted to text Eva. I was lost in my head until I remembered that Tessa was still lying next to me.

I looked over at her and she ran her hand through her hair. With the movement I noticed her arm again. I squinted to get a better look but between my blurred vision and the dim lighting in the room, I couldn't see it well.

"What's on your arm?" I asked, just to break the awkward

silence that was forming. I was tired, and the room was getting blurrier. I wasn't sure if I was blacking out or not.

I just want to leave.

I was about to start crying when her response brought me up short, completely snapping me out of my spiraling state.

"Scars." Her voice was shallow and barely audible.

Scars? "Scars?"

"Yeah," she said with a long sigh.

I thought about this for a moment. "How did you get them?" I asked, forgetting the tears that were so close just a moment before.

She rolled towards me. She looked bored. "I gave them to myself. Wow I'm drunk. Hey are you sure you don't want to have sex?"

"Wait what? You gave them to yourself?" I looked from her to her arm, confused.

Why would someone give themselves scars? Why would someone hurt themselves like that?

The idea had really never occurred to me. But then I heard that voice in my head.

You know exactly why.

She handed me her arm casually. I looked closer at it. White lines covered her arm, all tight together just above her wrist. Some looked red, mad, and angry. I touched them gently, tracing them with my fingers and she shivered softly, arching her back and taking back her arm.

"Yes."

"Why?"

We laid there in a stranger's bed looking at the ceiling, both of us completely still, completely silent. Finally, when she spoke, her words were barely a whisper.

"Because it takes the pain away." She took a deep breath and once more, even slower and softer, said, "It takes the pain away." Her words fell onto me like gentle rain on a chilly day.

I didn't respond. I didn't know what to say.

What does that mean? Why did she tell me that? It takes the pain away? What pain does it take away?

That's when the door burst open and Brandon, the guy who had brought me all the drinks, fell through the doorway.

Tessa sat up, "What the fuck?!" she yelled. She jumped off the bed and grabbed her clothes. Disregarding the fact that she was nearly naked, she ran out of the room, dodging past Brandon who was now on the floor groaning.

When Brandon collected himself, he sprang up. "Hey Garraway," he said cheerfully and grinned. "Thought you might need some help. Honestly, I still don't know who she is but your buddy Mike said Ashley said no sex in the beds." He let loose an intoxicated howl of laughter, but stopped when he looked around and saw my clothes on the floor. "Oh NO! Did you have sex with her? Was I too late?! Have I failed my mission?!"

I sat there, propped up on my elbows, mouth dumbly dropped open. I cleared my throat. "What? No!" I stammered.

"Pheew. Definitely for the best. The royal day drinkers will be pleased. Welp," he said, a little awkwardly, now aware that he and I were the only two in the room and I was almost naked, "I guess I'll leave you to it." He laughed again and walked out of the room, but poked his head back in just a moment later. "Door shut? Leave it open?"

"Close it, please," I said. He did and I fell down on the bed and stared at the ceiling. I laid motionless for a long while. The girl's words echoed in my head. *It takes the pain away...* I didn't remember falling asleep.

III

The next morning, I woke up to grogginess and a splitting headache. Despite this, my mind raced.

Her arm. Her scars. What did she even do? What did she use? How exactly did it take the pain away? What pain was she feeling? Was it the same pain I feel inside of me?

I wanted to talk to Tessa. I needed to talk to her. But she left before there was light in the sky, wanting nothing to do with me.

The remaining people from the party were in the kitchen. Everyone, it seemed, had expected to sleep there and had brought pajamas to change into. As I walked in Mike got up and clapped me on the back.

"Dodged a bullet last night, huh, Garraway?" he said cheerfully.

"What do you mean?" I asked, wincing at his touch. An earthquake of pain rippled through my body. "Could I get some water?"

Mike barked a laugh and got me a glass. "Well, let's just say you don't want to get mixed up with Tessa. Glad to hear you didn't sleep with her. All sorts of stories. Sleeps with every guy she gets her hands on. And she's crazy."

"Huh." I said in response. I drained the glass of water and Mike filled it back up for me.

Maybe a bit misunderstood, I thought.

One of the girls at the kitchen table chimed in, "You have to be if you've already had an abortion and you're barely 18." She wore a gray sweatshirt and pajama pants that were covered in Superman logos.

"Oh, shut up," said another girl at the table. She blew long red curls out of her face with one big breath to reveal dim green eyes. "That's just a rumor. If you really want to know, ask her. And don't be mean," she said to Mike. "We don't judge you for all the stupid shit you do."

The girl with Superman PJs just rolled her eyes and turned as Mike started up again, grabbing and shaking my shoulders--causing yet another tremor of pain inside of me.

"Thank god for that," he smiled. "I'm sad we didn't see more of you, Garraway. Tessa dragged you away right before we rallied troops last night and I guess Brandon over here nearly broke down the door to save you. Had to send him in on a royal quest. A knight in shining armor." He paused, "Well maybe not shining armor..." He trailed off thinking, "A knight in off brand, second-hand armor is more like it."

I looked around the kitchen to the people chuckling and shaking their heads at Mike.

"Mike?" I asked and gestured to the general group. "Can you re-introduce me? I'm terrible with names. I do know Brandon though. He and I became... acquainted last night." I managed a weak smile.

Brandon, who wore a Disney "Hakuna Matata" t-shirt and blue flannel pajamas, grinned and wriggled his finger at me. "I love saving a damsel in distress," he joked.

"Introducing all of the misfit toys!" Mike announced grandly and started pointing out people in the room. There was Julie, Veronica,

Matt, Brandon again, Elizabeth and Taylor. "Oh," Mike said, pointing to the girl walking in from the bathroom, "and you know Ashley. Her house. Also, you may have met at my New Year's Party. I held her hair while she was puking her face off. Like a gentleman."

"Oh, shut up, Mike," Ashley scoffed, walking to him kissing him on the cheek and then giving the spot where she kissed a little slap. "I'm Ashley. It's nice to officially meet you, David. Sorry about Tessa - I honestly don't really know her that well. She asked to hang out kind of out of nowhere so I just invited her. And thank you for not having sex in my sister's bedroom." She wore baggy sweatpants that looked like they belonged to Mike and her brown hair was held up in a haphazard bun. "But if you slept naked for whatever reason, please tell me. Not judging, just promised my sister she would have clean sheets when she returned."

I looked at Ashley wearily. "I slept with my shirt off but that was it. Nothing too dangerous was exposed."

Ashley shrugged and casually said, "I might give them a wash, no offense. It's what I would want if the tables were turned."

"Do what you gotta do. Well it's really nice meeting all of you," I offered, steering the conversation away from me. "Again." I added awkwardly.

Mike smiled broadly. "And together," he said theatrically gesturing to the group of half dead and hungover people in the kitchen, "we are the DAY DRINKERS!"

The toaster dinged, punctuating Mike's announcement. Julie put her hands over her ears, Veronica put her face into her hands, and the others loudly protested and booed Mike.

"Stop calling us that, Mike," Elizabeth said as she walked to the toaster. She was short with brown hair and light brown eyes. She wore baggy gray sweatpants and a red sweater and she moved around the kitchen by sliding around on her big, comfy looking socks. She grabbed the now toasted bread, cut them all in half, lazily buttered them and started distributing slices to the people around her.

Taylor, the curly haired redhead, chewed on her piece of toast and complained, "When have we ever even drank during the day? The name doesn't make any sense." She rolled her eyes at Mike and turned to me. "It's nice to meet you, David."

"Oh, come on! It sounds cool!" Mike protested.

"Does it?" Ashley asked. "It makes us sound like a bunch of alcoholics."

Mike threw up his arms dramatically. "But we are, aren't we?" He looked around the room for anyone to contradict him. "We're a bunch of emotionally unstable high schoolers who use alcohol to deal with all the angst and everything else our chemically imbalanced brains throw at us!"

"I am quite stable, thank you very much," said Elizabeth and she let loose a loud yawn.

"Says the girl who cried in the bathroom for an hour last night," Matt chuckled and shook his head. He had long black hair that was sticking out in all sorts of directions. He leaned back and put his feet on Elizabeth's lap.

"Well I only cried because Julie started crying!" Elizabeth said, pushing Matt's legs off her lap. When he put them back, she pinched his toe and rolled her eyes but didn't push them off again.

"I only started crying because Brandon was being an ass," Julie whined and Matt and Elizabeth burst into laughter.

"Hey," Brandon said loudly. "I'm sorry, babe, but I was busy trying to save our new friend here from the wrath of Ashley. A royal Day Drinkers quest! It's not easy breaking into rooms and carding into locks you know. I almost broke my debit card. Besides, as soon as I was told David needed a knight in beautiful, gleaming, shining armor, thank you very much," he put his chin up proudly and then looked solemnly back at Julie, "I had to leave you." She sarcastically glared at him and pursed her lips.

Veronica who had a gothy vibe to her chimed in, "And I had to take care of both of them. They got tears on my new shirt. Brandon, you're a dumbass and I hate you. Now that I think about it, I hate all of you. And Mike, just because you feel neglected by your parents doesn't mean you have to drag us down into your alcoholic gutter."

"You love us," Mike said, and Veronica rolled her eyes in concession. He then turned to me, "You see what a hot mess we are? But we are a hot mess together! The DAY DRINKERS!" Everyone booed and laughed this time. "Who wants to watch Lord of the Rings and eat greasy food all day?" Everyone raised their hands. "David? You in?"

I looked at him and then at the rest of this hungover motley crew.

Who the hell are these people?

"Yeah, sure," I said. "What else am I doing?" A small cheer went through the little day drinker's crew.

The Day Drinkers distracted me for the next handful of hours, keeping my mind from wandering. I felt comfortable with them. They showed me that I wasn't the only shitshow our age and that I wasn't alone. I had much more in common with them than my old perfect friends. It was refreshing and I felt relaxed around them--I even almost felt happy.

But behind that comfort, behind that brief feeling of okayness, my true feelings lurked in the shadows of my mind. In those shadows, Tessa's voice repeated itself over and over and over again, just waiting for my little reprieve to end.

IV

The car ride home was complete agony. Having turned on my phone to dozens of angry texts from my mom, I eventually left the day drinkers. Like walking through a portal, as soon as I left the house, I felt all of my distracted happiness vanish. Every inch that brought me closer to my house, the sadness, the anger, the dark cloud in my mind all bore down upon me.

My mom was waiting for me in the kitchen. "Where the hell have you been? You. Are. Grounded! That means you do not leave this house under any circumstance! From here on out, unless you're driving to school, you don't get to use the car. Give me the goddamn keys right now." She was already yelling.

I felt the heat rising in me and I waited for her to take a breath. "You quite done? May I go to my room and feel ashamed yet?" I snarled, throwing the keys on the kitchen table. A fog settled on my mind.

"You ungrateful little shit. How dare you talk to me like that! Who are you?" she roared. "You are grounded for a month. So help me god if you leave this house again!"

"What are you going to do? Ground me for two months? Ground me for the rest of my fucking life? I can't wait to get out of this hellhole!" I screamed back at her.

"And where are you going to go, David? Where the hell are you going to go?" She was shaking with anger and slammed her hands on the kitchen table. "I got a call from your guidance counselor saying that your teachers are worried about your grades! Mr. Meyers has signed you in late countless times! You're not doing your homework! You're not putting in any effort whatsoever! You think colleges will accept you if you start failing classes? What has gotten into you, David? Who are you? You're like a stranger! You hide in your room and are rude and disrespectful all the time!" I walked past her, out of the kitchen and towards the stairs. "Don't you dare walk away from me! Don't you dare! Come back here right now!" I didn't stop. "This conversation is not over! David!" She yelled after me but didn't follow.

I slammed my bedroom door. The force of it shook my bedroom walls. I fell onto my bed and began to cry. A minute later, I heard the crash as some unfortunate dish hit a wall followed by my mom's own sobs. I put a pillow over my head to block out the sound.

It was a while before I stopped crying. I lay in bed, staring at my ceiling. I heard a small knock at the door and before I could react, I heard it click open and my sister spoke.

"You know she cried herself to sleep last night?" Steph's voice was soft but clear. Any anger I still had died away. "She and Dad are always yelling about you. Dad convinced her not to take your phone away... just in case the next time you leave you might actually get in trouble and need to call for help."

I remained silent.

"Just thought you might want to know." She hesitated and said gently, "I'm here if you... want to talk or something." And she left my room, shutting the door behind her.

Hours passed. I didn't move. My bladder ached with the need to pee. Still, I didn't leave my room. The day dimmed and night took over the sky. I stayed in bed. Eventually, I heard footsteps come up the stairs and go into my parent's bedroom. I continued to wait. What did I wait for? I didn't even know. But the voice inside my head did. It was the same voice that had been whispering, chanting, the same thing over and over and over again the entire day.

"It takes the pain away. It takes the pain away. It takes the pain away..."

The clock's red neon numbers showed midnight when I sat up. I quietly left my room and carefully walked to the bathroom--the pain in my bladder had become unbearable.

When I returned, I didn't go to my bed but instead walked slowly to my desk and turned the lamp on. I reached for my journal and placed it in front of me. I stared at it but didn't touch it again. Instead, I reached into my drawer and after searching for a moment, pulled out my small red Swiss Army knife. Concealed within it: a bottle opener, a screwdriver, and other little things that folded out. I was only interested in one. The knife. It was a short blade, but terribly sharp. I placed it next to the journal and stared. I reached for it, but then drew back. I stood up and took off the long sleeve button-up from the night before and replaced it with a simple black t-shirt. I sat back down. I stared.

It takes the pain away...

My desk lamp's light glistened off the blade. I didn't like it. I stood up again and grabbed a candle from my dresser. I had never used it before, but it was red and seemed appropriate. I picked up a little box of matches I kept in my drawer, struck one and I lit the wick.

I turned off the lamp and sat and observed the knife. The candle's flame flickered and reflected off the metal. I liked it better. It was mesmerizing. The candle's wax began to melt and pool.

It takes the pain away.

It was more than a whispered chant now.

It takes the pain away.

The voice was growing louder. I stood up and paced my room. My hands clenched and unclenched and clenched and unclenched. My eyes were brimming with tears. As I walked in a lopsided circle around my room, the glisten of the knife grew as my vision blurred.

It takes the pain away!

I hit my head with my hand hard, trying to knock the voice out of my head. As if in retaliation, my head shook.

It takes the pain away!

It was shouting now. Tears streamed down my face and my lopsided circle turned into random and frantic zigzags.

IT TAKES THE PAIN AWAY!

All I could do was listen to Tessa's words, but they were my words now, it was my voice that screamed them over and over. I couldn't take it anymore. I threw myself back into my chair. I grabbed the knife and slashed three cuts into my arm.

The sharp metal parted my skin and thick beads of blood began to gather and stream down my arm. The sting sparked electricity up my arm and I gasped. My hand started shaking. I dropped the knife and it clattered onto the desk. "Shit," I said, thinking someone might wake up. I reached for the knife but knocked the candle over, it rocked and splattered hot wax across my desk and journal. The flame went out, leaving me in darkness.

I frantically fumbled for my lamp and clicked it. In its light, I could see my arm. They were shallow cuts, but there still was more blood than I expected. I grabbed tissues off my desk and pressed them against my arm. The pressure sent another sting through my body and I let out a quiet moan. I pressed my mouth into my right shoulder to muffle my sobs. Not knowing what to do, I rushed to my bed. I laid there, crying and shaking. I didn't remember falling asleep.

CONSEQUENCES

I

David wiped away a tear from his face. He hadn't said anything for a few minutes and Lily waited patiently for him, watching him closely. Her pen kept going down to her clipboard but stopping, not wanting to break the silence with its scribbling.

David's left arm was pinned to his chest, as if to protect it from his own words. He looked down at the black socks that covered his feet. He took a deep breath, and then another.

Eventually, David composed himself, faked a chuckle, then sniffled. "Shit, sorry about that," he said, puffy eyed. "It feels like I've been crying for the past six months straight."

"There is no reason to apologize, David. None at all," Lily said. "Would you like a break? Maybe stretch our legs?" She looked at her watch. Nearly three hours had gone by.

David nodded. "That might be nice. It does only get worse from here."

David and Lily walked for a few more minutes in a not uncomfortable silence and then returned to the room.

"What's he like?" David asked.

Lily gave him a confused look. "Who?"

"Your partner. What's he like?"

Lily was a little taken aback. "Well," she said, "he's quite amazing. He's an artist. A talented one, too."

"What kind of art?" David asked.

"Lately he has been going out and doing more landscape works though. He loves nature. He wants to show that love is within nature, and by loving nature we are actually loving ourselves. His new project is to try and show that."

"Wow, he actually sounds kind of cool," David admitted.

Lily raised an eyebrow at this. "You sound surprised."

"Well..." David began, "the way you told me earlier today that he made you make breakfast this morning... I don't know, it kind of sounded like he... was a jerk." David's voice was high pitched and his face had turned a shade of red.

Lily just stared at David for a moment, appearing to take in his words. Then, she threw her head back and let out a laugh. It rang out and filled the room. "No," she said, "that's not what I meant at all when I said that. I guess it might sound strange since you don't know him, or our relationship together."

"Sorry, sorry," David stammered. "I shouldn't have assumed."

"It's okay, David." She said, smiling at him. "It was romantic because he never lets me cook. Actually, he insists on cleaning and cooking. It was a treat to cook for him this morning." Her smile was turned into a small knowing smirk. "Not what you expected?"

"Well, no." David said and gave a small, embarrassed smile.

Lily shrugged. "He likes taking care of me and knows how hard I work. Frankly, it's really nice to get home to a cooked meal and a clean kitchen. I have it pretty well."

"I think you and Leland would like each other a lot," David said and then added awkwardly, "Team queen."

Lily blinked and gave him a confused smile. "Well, why don't we get back to it. Are you ready to continue?"

"I think so. Questions? Comments? Concerns?"

Lily cleared her throat and put her pen to paper. "So, that was the first time you harmed yourself? You had never thought about it before Tessa told you about it at the party?"

"Correct."

"That voice you were hearing. The voice that, as you put it, whispers in your head. Can you tell me more about it?"

"Yeah, sure. It was my own voice, obviously. But I guess talking about it now I can see that it wasn't really me. It sounded like me, but it wasn't me. It was the depression talking—or whatever. At the time, I did think it was me. My own thoughts. I call it 'the voice' because..." David trailed off. "Because I'm embarrassed I didn't have control. It was me. It was my voice. I hurt myself, it was me and I'm ashamed... I don't want it to be me. Does that make sense?" He let out a long shaky sigh. "I'm still figuring most of this out as I go along. I'm still trying to remember too."

"That makes sense, David." Lily said and gave him a sorrowful look. She made on last note. "Okay, ready when you are."

David leaned back in his chair. "Let's start with the next morning. The really bad thing with...uh, cutting... is that it does help. Or no, it doesn't help but it makes you feel again. Sort of. At first at least. Then it makes everything bad. Makes everything one million times worse. It really was the beginning of the end. I just didn't understand it *yet. What that girl Tessa said - she didn't tell me what happened after the pain went away. I guess I know why there were so many scars on her arm. Once you start, you can't stop."*

II

When I opened my eyes the next morning, I knew something was wrong. Or... not wrong but different. Something was different. I sat up and winced as my sheets unstuck from the dried blood on my arm. Luckily, they were blue, so the stains didn't really show. It took a second of staring at the stains before I remembered what happened last night. And then it all came crashing down on me.

I jumped out of bed and the cuts on my arm yelped in pain. I looked curiously down at my forearm and gently touched one of the red lines. A little shock ran up my arm and I shivered, breaking into goose bumps all over. I walked over to my desk and stared at the little red Swiss Army knife. The sharp silver tip was coated with a thin layer of crimson. It was there, perfectly still. Not waiting... just sitting.

I stood there and did a mental evaluation. Nothing. No voice, no chanting—nothing. Only my own thoughts in my head, and they weren't spiraling, or swirling or flooding or anything. Then I felt for the hot pressure that had been built up inside of me for so long, making me feel like a nail gun connected to a tank of compressed air, ready to shoot at anyone who dared speak to me. It was gone too. I didn't feel deflated and even more shockingly, I didn't feel like I was going to explode either.

This dramatic change and the mere memory of what I did sent waves of fear through me. I didn't understand what was happening. The images of what had happened the night before flashed behind my eyelids every time I blinked, like bright lightning in a dark sky. But the voice in my head was gone--its absence was unnerving.

What the hell is happening? I thought.

Silence was the response. My mind was quiet.

I maneuvered a long-sleeved t-shirt and walked downstairs. Every time I moved my left arm, the shirt brushed up against my cuts and sent fiery stings up my arm, reminding me that they were there.

My dad was sitting at the kitchen table and looked up when I walked in.

"David, we need to talk." His voice was low and serious.

I glanced at him, eyeing the pot of coffee on the counter, freshly brewed by the smell of it. "Yeah sure. Mind if I steal some coffee first?"

He looked at me as if I was a stranger. It was more words than I had spoken to him in all of two weeks.

"Help yourself." He watched me as I grabbed a mug from the cupboard and poured myself some. He cleared his throat. "What you pulled yesterday, David. It was unacceptable. Not okay. At all. You can't speak to your mother that way. You need to apologize to her. She didn't even want to be in the house today. That's how upset she is." He picked up his mug and realized it was empty.

I walked over, grabbed the mug out of his hand, refreshed it for him, and handed it back steaming. He nodded a confused thanks, unsure of what was happening. It was probably the most he had seen of me too.

"I'm sorry," I said, taking a sip from my mug. "I shouldn't have done that. Just needed to, you know, get out for a bit." I yawned. My dad continued to look at me. The idea of speaking to my mother didn't seem great, but it didn't trigger me into rage either. It was an interesting change. When I lowered my cup, the cuts on my arm flared as I awkwardly set it down.

"David, it doesn't matter if you needed to get out. You need to respect our rules." He put down his coffee. "This is our house. You are our son. Apologize to your mother. You're still lucky you have your phone. You're lucky you aren't grounded until summer. You're lucky you are grounded forever." He took a breath and sighed. "We don't know what has gotten into you lately, but it needs to change. I've never seen Bev so upset." He rubbed his face with his hands. "She threw a plate after your yelling match yesterday?" He paused then, taking another long deep breath. The man looked exhausted. "David, we are so worried about you. Your mother is as confused as hell. Jesus, David, I'm confused too." His face was serious, he stared intently at me. Then the seriousness dropped away. "David," he said much more quietly. "We love you."

Guilt and shame filled me as tears threatened. Without that voice in my head to distract me, I could see the damage I had been causing on his tired face and hear it in his exhausted voice. I blinked and saw a flash of the candlelight flickering off the blade.

I cleared my throat, "I'm sorry, Dad." I said, and even to my surprise, I meant it. "School has been getting to me I guess. I'm gonna go catch up on homework." I paused, and then cleared my throat. "But I don't want to talk to her. I can't even be in the same room with her without her getting mad at me."

He looked like he was going to say something and opened his mouth but then closed it, apparently changing his mind. I walked out of the kitchen, leaving him.

I actually did my homework for the first time since I didn't know how long. It wasn't half-assed, it was complete. It did take the entire weekend though. I was so far behind it was scary but I could think, for the first time in such a long time, I could actually focus without wanting to give up and hide in my room, crying myself to sleep.

At school, other students gave me strange looks when I greeted them in the hallway—well "greeted" might be a stretch. It was more that I made brief eye contact and gave weak smiles. It had been so long since I went out of my way to be social in any aspect—aside from texting Mike, of course. By the end of the week, things were far from back to normal but I was in full damage control mode, my mind was clear and I searched desperately for ways to regain anything of what my grades once resembled—all the while my mother's warning about college fueling me.

I spoke to almost every one of my teachers and asked them how best to catch up. They were doubtful at first, thinking I was being forced to go to them. Most of them gave me extra work and to their surprise, I got most of it back to them, mostly correct and as complete as I could manage. This gave me some breathing room.

I still hadn't spoken to Leland, Charlie, or Eva. I guessed that if I went to them and apologized, they would take me back, maybe not at first, but eventually. I couldn't though. I still felt like I didn't want them in my life, still felt like they were too good for me and that they shouldn't waste their time on me. In class, I politely ignored them. In homeroom SLAM, we were professionals. Leland was surprised when I didn't fight her every word and instead supported the things she said and nodded along. If anything, it made them more hesitant of me.

II

In the week that followed, I did my best to halt my C's and maybe one or two D's in their painful decay. During that week or however long this lasted, I felt okay. I would see Mike at lunch and at least once during the week we would go over to one of the infamous Day Drinker's houses. I told my parents that I was going to study groups and they believed me, since my mother was notified by some of my

WHERE IS MY MIND?

teachers that I was picking it back up—the annoyingly chipper Mr. Holden acting as the pestering messenger bird. Maybe they were hopeful that whatever it was that happened to me was finally coming to an end and that things were going to become normal or even good again.

At our Day Drinker meets, we would do homework together—sometimes at least. All of them were surprisingly smart, not top of their class smart like my old friends but competent and not annoying about it. We joked about hating our lives and laughed at each other for being dramatic or overly emotional. We could talk about anything. Almost everything.

I didn't tell them about cutting. I didn't tell anyone. I thought that once they healed, the scars would fade and I would never have to think about them again. Oh, how wrong I was. A week? Maybe two? My break of clarity was short lived and soon my heart and mind sank back down into confused unhappiness. I begged myself to not let it happen. I told myself that I was in control of my own mind and that I wouldn't get bad again. But no.

That haunting voice began whispering again and the storm cloud dawned, threatening thunder and lightning. The monster in the shadows lurked.

I tried to not cut. I really did. But it came on so much faster, the urges to hurt myself so much stronger and this time. It was because I knew the way to take the pain away. I didn't know what else to do. Of course I cut again—I felt like I had to. Every time I did it, it left me bloody and shaking. But it also kept me going. The problem was that every time I cut myself, the next time had to be deeper, more was required just to get back to the same point of sluggish okayness. I felt like an addict. I was an addict. I would get my fix, feel better, go into damage control mode, have hope, lose hope, fall deeper into darkness, cut deeper into myself. And with every cut, a part of me died.

When I got bad, my house would turn into a war zone. My mom and I would constantly scream at each other for no reason. My sister would hide, my dad would try to comfort my mom afterwards, and I would always retreat back to my room. My mom would always win, but then again, there was no winning. She just got the last word, she just yelled the loudest and with every word exchanged I got worse, I became more broken.

After the screaming stopped, my sister would try and come to me. I think she was as scared as they were. She knew something was terribly wrong but, like my mother, like my father and all my old friends, she didn't know what to do or what was happening.

"David," her quiet voice would come through the door to my bedroom. "David, are you okay? Do you want to talk?" I would be laying there, tears staining my pillow, unable to think about anything except my hatred for everything, my desolated and drained hope for my future and how much my arm burned and itched to be cut open.

On the weekends I would sneak out since I was grounded until the end of upcoming summer, quite literally. I would lock my door, climb out of my window, get onto the roof and climb down a tree that leaned right up against the edge of our house. A loyal Day Drinkers would always be there, waiting for my escape—the get-away driver. Then we would get drunk. We would cry. I would cry. They would just say, "David's having another episode," as I sobbed in the corner, itching at my arm. My nights always ended in tears. I don't think that any of the Day Drinkers knew that I was hurting myself but they knew that something was wrong. Taylor, or Brandon or even Elizabeth would talk to me and console each time.

In those days, drinking was the only way I was able to fall asleep. Thankfully, everyone seemed to have an older brother or sister and getting alcohol wasn't a problem. So even when I wasn't with my Day Drinkers, I would find myself curled up with a bottle of something terrible, eyes swollen, slowly drifting off to sleep each night.

***

David shifted in his chair. "This is where my memory really starts to get spotty. Where everything just started to blur together. The drinking didn't help and my depression was getting out of control, so I guess that doesn't really help either... but there was one night I remember now."

***

I had left a party, not the Day Drinker's, not a party of anyone I really knew. I was bad that night, and I was especially drunk. Earlier that day I had found the hiding place my mom was keeping my keys and took my car. I didn't care anymore. So away from the party I stumbled and I drove off into the night. I was crying. It hadn't even been a week since the last time I cut, four very shallow cuts into my arm. A quick fix. But its effects didn't last as long as I thought they would and as I drove, dark thoughts plagued and controlled my mind. Alcohol, a friend and ally, aiding and exaggerating my depression.

***

"I remember sitting at a stop sign in front of a major road. The speed limit was 50. And for a minute I just watched the cars fly past in front of me."

***

I knew how easy it would be to just pull out in front of an oncoming car and let it take me and put an end to the suffering--my horrible excuse of a life. And I did. I pulled right in front of oncoming headlights. I heard the horn blaring and I started to scream. I was ready for it to take me.

But the realization of potentially killing whoever hit me shocked my system. I felt my foot slam the gas and I turned the wheel wildly. It all happened in the space of maybe five seconds. Then I was safely in the right lane. The truck flew by me and it was over. I sped away, crying uncontrollably, absolutely horrified that I almost hurt another person.

I went home and, like the starving addict I was, got my fix and let a river of drunken tears guide me to sleep.

At some point, my admission letters came back. I had gotten into college. My mother opened each letter before I got to them and left them on the kitchen table. I didn't care that she opened them. I was just so relieved. To my surprise, I had gotten into almost every college I applied to--all my low hanging fruit fell right into my lap. Thankfully my grades when I applied were good enough to get me in. I took each into my room and cried tears of relief as I read them. The acceptances were one of the very few things that had kept me going, a hope of a better, maybe even happier future. I was going to college. I picked one, accepted their invitation to freedom and...

***

"That basically sums up my March and April," David shivered. "Or at least I think it was March and April. Honestly, I can't really... time wasn't something that I kept track of. I can't tell you when those things happened. I have absolutely no idea. Right now, I'm just remembering things that come to me at this point. Like I said, everything is just so blurring and foggy."

Lily sat there looking thoughtfully at David for a long moment. Her pen had been rapidly flying across the page as David spoke but now it sat in her idle hand. David had grown used to the soft scribbles as he spoke and now, without it, the room seemed void of noise and especially empty.

"Was that the first time you thought of suicide?" Lily asked, her voice was soft.

David recoiled at the word.

"Suicide," he repeated slowly. "This might sound strange, but I don't think I even knew what suicide was." He looked down at his hands, then at his arm. It was still covered by his long sleeve shirt. "Or I knew the general concept, but I don't think I thought about it then. That might have been the moment where the seed was planted, the general concept of... dying... on purpose," he paused to take a shaky breath, "to, uh, you know, take the pain away."

Lily made a note and asked, "How often do you think you harmed yourself?"

"I honestly don't know. Once a few weeks maybe? I really didn't start cutting deep until towards the end. But the more I did it... well it made me need to... you know, uh, hurt myself more often."

"And no one noticed? Your arm?" Lily asked.

"They did. I can talk more about that," David said somberly.

"You haven't read from your journal in a little while," Lily prompted. It wasn't a question, merely a statement holding all sorts of questions.

David looked down at the journal. It lay on the floor looking menacing and evil.

He sighed. "I haven't. Would you like to hear from it?"

"I would," Lily admitted.

"Well, I haven't read these, but let the fun begin I guess," David said, sighing and picked up the journal. He went to where he left off, read a few lines and then skipped a couple pages. Lily frowned at this.

"What did you just skip?" She asked.

David looked up. "Relax," he said, "it was just a boring one about me taking the pain away. It would be a waste of time, I already basically covered it. Don't need to relive it a third time."

"If you say so."

"Here we go," David said. "Don't judge me when I start crying."

THE JOURNAL ENTRIES

I

Dear whoever,

I don't know how to explain it. It's like a wave, or maybe an incoming tide. I feel so good, but then I don't. It sneaks up on me. I don't know I'm underwater until I'm already drowning.

After I cut, the clouds part and I am graced with sunlight. I can breathe, I can think, I can hope again. I don't even notice when the clouds come back, that's how subtle, how insidious it is. I find myself waist deep in water. When I notice, it's too late. A monster wave is already cascading down on me. When that happens, there is only one way out.

It's a pressure—an invisible weight pushing down and pressing down onto my temples. I am exhausted and weak all the time. I don't want to think, I don't want to speak, move, feel. But within that feeling of not wanting to feel, I feel everything. Everything is too much. I can feel the weight of everyone and everything. But at the same time it's like I feel nothing at all. I feel numb. I know that doesn't make any sense but not much of anything does anymore. I cry all the time and I just can't stop.

I want to hide. Hide from the world and from this terrible life. I need to escape this place, this house, this town. I'm mentally suffocating here and I know fresh air just waiting for me. Somewhere, anywhere that isn't here.

DG

Dear whoever,

I feel like I could be alone forever. I like not being around people. I have learned that I am a burden. And the best thing I can do is to just be alone. There is something wrong with me. I am damaged goods—Please return to sender.

DG

Dear whoever,

I'm afraid to sleep. I try to avoid it. It's funny because I usually can't even fall asleep anyways. But when I do, I have nightmares. The demon inside of me takes control and runs rampant through my mind. Nowhere is safe anymore. I am so tired. I'm so scared.

DG

Dear whoever,

What am I doing with my life? All I do is drink now. It numbs me while at the same time sets a burning inside of me. My friends finally saw my scars. I wanted to cut at a party the other night and Taylor stopped me. She held me as I cried. She just kept telling me that I needed to stop - needed to stop hurting myself, to stop cutting. She doesn't understand. I can't stop. I need to, I want to. I am an addict and cutting is my drug. It is the only thing I feel anymore, or it helps me to feel. The pain and euphoria that comes with it is the only thing that wakes me from this… thing that I have become. What is more poisonous? The alcohol I drink or my soul?

DG

Dear whoever,

I hate myself so fucking much. So do my parents. They won't admit it though. Cowards. All my friends are cowards too. I hate Charlie. I hate Leland. I hate Eva. They stare at me in school. I can feel their condescending concern. Why don't they get that I don't want them to care about me anymore? I pushed them away out of love. I am nothing. I am absolutely nothing.

DG

Dear whoever,

I have become so good at lying. I can even laugh and smile now. I don't feel anything though. Lies just fall out of my lips. It's easier than breathing. Teachers, classmates, my parents. And it's so easy to pretend that I'm okay now. I walk around and look normal. No one can see that I'm drowning right in front of them. No one can see that I am empty. No one can hear my screams as I thrash underwater. But it has to be that way. So I'm not a burden to other people. They just don't understand that they would be better off without me. And so I lie. Lie about doing homework, or turning in papers, or "no I haven't been crying those are just my allergies," and "Yes, really, I'm fine! I've actually never been better!" And lie and lie and lie. My life is a lie, lying is what I do. It's all so easy. So why is living so hard?

DG

Dear whoever,

Sometimes I fantasize about having a family. This only makes me cry more. Because every time I get to naming my children, I remember that no one would love me. No one would love something so broken. I am poison. All I do is destroy. I am a scar that will never heal. I will never find love because I will push it away before it gets too close. I don't deserve love anyways. But it's nice to think about, sometimes at least.

DG

Dear whoever,

I've been thinking about killing myself. The idea of drifting off in the snow sounds peaceful. The snow is basically all gone though, so I might wait until next winter… but that is so far away. I don't know. I just want peace. This world cannot give me that anymore. Not anymore. I went online and there is some helpful stuff. Some real interesting stuff…

DG

Dear whoever,

I am so tired. I'm just so fucking tired. I don't want to live anymore. There is so much pain and nothing takes it away anymore. I am a burden to everything I touch, to everything that looks at me. I just want to die.

DG

II

David closed the book and closed his eyes.

"A nice short one, that last, huh?" He wiped his face and forced out a laugh. Lily sat there and let him collect himself. "The funny thing is that I don't remember writing a single one of these. Not one." David turned slightly and looked out the window. "There are two entries left. Two real fun ones, I'm guessing. But like I said," he turned back to Lily, "that basically wraps up March and April. It's funny, I would have thought I would have written more about getting into college. Or the Day Drinkers." He choked out something that resembled a laugh and a cry. "It's like a stranger wrote this. A crazy lunatic. I don't remember any of this." He wiped more tears from his eyes.

"It's okay that you don't remember, David. It really is okay. You are doing such a great job but I'm wondering if we should pace ourselves. We can always pick this up tomorrow. I don't want you to become overwhelmed. We have already covered more than was expected for today," Lily said gently, clearing her throat.

David frowned at this. "I would like to finish," he said, and there was icy determination in his voice. "I'm so close and I don't think that I will be able to start again if we stop today."

Lily looked at him thoughtfully and then she nodded. "Then let's finish. Where are we starting from?"

"Before we go on, can I just say something?" David asked, looking down to his hands.

"Yes of course, David. You can say anything you want to." Lily gave him a reassuring smile.

David thought for a minute, clenching and unclenching his hands. "I just feel so stupid."

"How do you mean, David?" Lily flipped a page on her clipboard and readied her pen.

"I have nothing to complain about. I feel so stupid when I'm talking about this because it's complaining about nothing. Like nothing bad has ever happened to me and suddenly I'm the saddest, most pathetic person in the universe."

"David--" Lily began, but was cut off as David continued.

"I hurt myself, and cry all the time. Why? Because I'm sad for no reason? Nothing bad has ever happened to me! I have no reason to be this fucking sad but I am and it's not fair. Other people have the right to be this sad, this pathetic, but I don't. Charlie and Leland... they have more to complain about than me. They have real problems."

Lily straightened up in her chair. *"First of all, depression isn't just getting randomly sad, David. It is a very serious and legitimate mental illness. The problem you're having is that you just can't see it. Depression isn't a tangible thing. It's not like a broken bone that you can go to the doctor's for. It is a much more complex problem that requires just as much time and attention and healing.*

"Second, comparing problems will never solve anything. When you compare something you're dealing with to another person's problems, you are minimalizing yourself. That's only hurting yourself. Not only that, but it's nearly impossible to help another person with their problems if you can't help yourself with your own. Saying you don't deserve to be that sad isn't going to make you less sad, it's only going to make it worse and make you feel more guilt. Contrary to popular belief, helping yourself isn't selfish, although it may feel like that sometimes. It's actually a remarkably selfless thing to do, and that's because it puts you in a better position to help others. Just think about all the confusion and harm your depression has brought into your life. You said it yourself--it has affected the lives of everyone close to you. They were confused and scared, and a lot of your relationships have taken a toll because of it." Lily looked David hard in the eyes. *"And I know you didn't know what was going on. I know that you didn't even know what depression was while you were experiencing it. Right now, right here, just by talking to*

me, you are being selfless. You are putting yourself in a better position to heal all of those relationships that have been affected by your depression."

David was crying again. "I've hurt a lot of people... I don't even know if I can face them. Not ever."

"Take it from me," Lily assured, "some people will have a hard time understanding it. I was depressed back in college and still sometimes now. But when I was at an extremely low point, I hurt my sister very badly. I pushed her away and to this day, our relationship isn't the same. Trust me, David, I understand."

David wiped his eyes for what felt the millionth time and looked up. "You have depression?"

"It's much more common than people think. People who don't know they have it can go undiagnosed. Which is what happened to you and what is happening to so many people all over. This is why it is so important to talk about. Especially since it isn't something you can see. It's hard for people without depression to understand how terrible it actually is. How hard it is to get out of bed some days, how hard it is to ask for help. And too many times we lose people to it."

"Was your depression bad?" David asked quietly.

"It was," Lily sighed. "I fortunately was taught about depression, anxiety and all about mental health in most of my college classes and had some pretty amazing friends who helped me get through some of my worst days. My therapist was great too. I got through it and I know you can too. And I wasn't alone, David. If I tried dealing with my depression by myself, I don't know if things would be the same. I had so much help. Asking for help isn't weak. It's strength. Even if it's just reaching out to talk to someone. It's being vulnerable and a lot more people need to get comfortable with doing that."

They sat in comfortable silence, David digesting her words.

"Why don't we stretch our legs again, and let's get you some water. Crying is very dehydrating, trust me." She gave him a warm smile. "When we get back, we can finish."

"That sounds great," David smiled back.

When they were back in their chairs, David put down his big cup of water and picked up his journal. He flipped to the second to last entry and smiled sadly at it. He then closed it and set it down.

"Before I dive back into that, let me start with one of the worst days I've had in my life."

"What happened?" Lily asked.

"Wait are you ready? Do you need to do anything before I start?"

"Nope, ready when you are."

"Well here we go then. Oh jeez," David said, thinking back, "shit really hit the fan. Let's just say, it was an especially bad day."

THE DECLINE

I

Let's just say, it was an especially bad day. It started when Deb from the office came and collected me from our homeroom. We were in the middle of a discussion with our SLAM group to finalize our end-of-year service project. We were going to pick up trash from a nearby beach and have a cookout afterwards—all the Slammers were pretty excited since it didn't really involve much work.

"David?" Deb asked, giving the open door to our classroom a soft knock as she poked her head in. Leland was just assigning each of the Slammers either a food item or a cleaning item to bring. I was sitting quietly next to her, pretending to listen by nodding along. At the sound of the knock, everyone in the room turned, except for me.

"Oh, so sorry to interrupt, I just need to steal David for the rest of homeroom." Her words hung in the air and my stomach felt like it was about to turn inside out.

I stood and walked out the door. I didn't bring my backpack with me since I was planning on cutting whatever this was as short as possible. I could feel everyone's eyes on me as I left. They knew I was going through some shit, even the freshmen. At that point, they knew I was only present during SLAM days because I had to be, not because I wanted to. I usually sat out of our icebreakers and discussions each week. Leland and Charlie let me do this since they were still slightly scared of me. Scared and confused because they still didn't understand the stranger I had become.

Despite the ever-warming temperatures, I still wore long-sleeved shirts to cover my arm. My arm was littered with small cuts: some bigger than others, some pale and white, some red and angry. I

146

would start at the top forearm and move my way down, and by the time I reached just before my wrist, the top cuts would (mostly) be healed and I was ready to start again. A vicious circle.

Sometimes I would roll my sleeves up without realizing what I was doing and would only realize when I absent-mindedly rubbed my arm and found it uncovered. But for the most part I kept them hidden. I had been trying to keep them as shallow as possible, but their effects weren't what they used to be. I was concerned that I was going to have to keep going deeper and deeper. By then, I was fully aware of how terrible it was. But I felt like I needed it. It was all that kept me mildly in control. It was the only thing I felt anymore.

I mournfully followed Deb down the mostly empty hall. Low and behold, she took me to the guidance counselor's office. I was in for another one of Mr. Holden's famous pep-talks it seemed. He and his dumb hair were waiting for me when we entered.

"David," Mr. Holden said brightly, "thanks for coming." He nodded a thanks to Deb and she departed. "Let's go to my office."

Without responding, I walked down the little hall lined with other offices for the other counselors. He followed me.

When I reached his door and saw what was waiting for me, I froze. I was about to turn around and run when I felt Mr. Holden's firm hand on my shoulder. Gently, he pushed me into his office.

No. No, no, no. What the hell is this? What are they doing here? My mind raced and I began to panic.

Inside the cramped room, my parents sat in two of his annoyingly comfortable chairs. They turned and looked at me as we entered.

"What is this?" I said, feeling the anger rise inside of me and my face grow red and hot.

"Why don't you sit down, David?" Mr. Holden said, shutting the door behind us and walking around his desk to take a seat. "I asked your parents to come in today. The three of us wanted to talk to you because we are worried about you. Someone has contacted us because they think you are harming yourself..."

I felt the pressure inside of me rise and rise and rise. I felt like I was burning. School was supposed to be a safe place away from my parents, away from my mother. They were speaking around me, but I couldn't hear. A darkness was taking over me. A thick fog covered my mind and my vision seemed to go in and out.

All I remembered hearing was "your grades," "failing," "in danger of not graduating," and "harming yourself." I could hear my own voice, my own furious yells, but it sounded echoed and distant like I was listening from a far-off place. I heard my mom yelling and my dad trying to calm her down. Mr. Holden kept telling everyone to "calm down," and "there's no need to yell."

I didn't remember anything else. One moment I was in Mr. Holden's office screaming and then the next moment I was sobbing in one of the bathroom stalls. Someone was knocking on a door and saying something. I straightened up, disoriented and exhausted. Then I realized that the person was banging on my the door and yelling, "David? David! Are you in there?"

How did I get here?

I wiped my eyes, trying to collect myself. I couldn't let anyone see me like this. "Yes," I managed to choke out, "what do you want? I'm fine." The tears wouldn't stop. My eyes stung and were so puffy I could barely see.

"David, it's Charlie. Please open the door."

Charlie? My confusion turned to cold hostility, "What the fuck do you want?"

"I just want to make sure you're okay," he said and concern poured from his voice. "You left your backpack in homeroom and I wanted to get it back to you." He hesitated. He sounded hurt, sounded desperate, but that only brought me grim satisfaction.

"Whatever," I said. "Just kick it under the door and leave."

He didn't kick it under. "I saw your parents leaving," he said softly. "They were crying."

"Woopty-fucking-doo."

"Your mom loves you, David." As his words hung in the air, I felt the pressure tearing through my head. The blackness threatened again. To my horror, he continued to speak. "She has been texting me non-stop. She doesn't know what is happening with you. Lee and I don't know what's happening to you. No one does. I told Mr. Holden that you were cutting yourself. I've seen your arm. Man, I didn't know what else to do. I'm sorry." As he said each word, the anger inside of me consumed me more and more. My vision went in and out and I felt like I was burning alive. "Please, Dave... we're all so worried."

My arm throbbed and my head felt like it was splitting down in two.

"Dave..."

Get the fuck out of here! "Get the fuck out of here!" I screamed.

Then everything went black again.

When I woke up again, I had my backpack clutched in my arms and my head rested on the divider wall. Someone was pulling at the stall door. Before I could start screaming again, whoever it was moved on to the next stall and went in. I heard them unzip their pants and sit down.

I stood up, unlocked the door and threw it open. I ran out of the bathroom and down the hall. A class period must have been in session since the hallways were deserted. I had no idea what time it was or where I was supposed to be. All I knew was I needed to get out, to leave. I ran down the nearest hall and slipped out the back entrance of the school. There were P.E. groups a little way off and I slowed to a fast walk in the direction of the senior parking lot, just so I wouldn't catch their attention.

When I got into my car I began crying again. Then I drove. I don't know for how long or for how far but I just kept driving. Eventually, I turned off a main road and onto a smaller back road. I pulled over, parked and fell asleep.

II

When I woke up, it was just getting dark.

How could she go there? How dare they go there! How could Charlie betray me like that!?

I slammed my hands on the wheel and thrashed around, punching my backpack, the roof, the horn, my body.

When I calmed, I started my car and drove off. It took me a while to figure out where I was but I eventually did and made my way back home.

It was dark when I pulled into the driveway and to my relief, no one was waiting for me in the kitchen when I walked in. The table was clear, except for an opened envelope and a tri-folded piece of paper which laid next to it.

I picked up the envelope. It was addressed to me from my college. The piece of paper felt cold in my hands and I was confused because they already sent the freshman information. I read it.

"Dear applicant,

Due to the steady decline of your overall GPA after your initial acceptance to our University, we regret to inform you that we are rescinding your acceptance..." I dropped the piece of paper and stood there, not comprehending what I was seeing. Then I picked it back up and kept reading, "enrollment is contingent upon maintaining academic achievement... an expectation for accepted students to preserve academic levels similar to those held upon their initial acceptance..."

I stood there looking at the letter for a long time. The more I stood staring at the white piece of paper, the more the words sunk into. Over and over I read it. I felt disconnected from myself, as if I came out of my body and watched my empty shell read and reread the letter.

Then I heard footsteps behind me.

"Are you happy with yourself? You embarrassed us all at school! You're failing and probably won't even graduate and now you lost college. YOU LOST COLLEGE!" When I didn't turn, she continued to yell. "Are you happy with yourself!? Are you proud? What's the plan, David? What are you doing?!"

My mother's words threw me back into my body. The reality hit me like a bullet. I wasn't going to college. I wasn't going anywhere. I had lost everything.

"I hate you," I whisper. I was still staring at the piece of paper on the table.

"What did you just say to me?" Her voice was low and menacing, daring me to answer her.

The more this new reality set in, the more anger I felt. I wanted to feel that darkness, to let it take me. I didn't want to remember. I didn't want to be there anymore. There wasn't anything left for me. I didn't have college, I didn't have friends, I didn't have a family. I had nothing. I deserved nothing. I reached for that voice of darkness and hate.

"I. HATE. YOU!" I screamed and wheeled on her.

My mom took a step back, her own anger faltering. It was the first time I had ever said those words to her. I could see the hurt on her face. The anger inside of me, the pressure, the clouds, the blackness, whatever it was relished in this small victory. Hate was not something used for family. I was taught that we did not hate family, because family came before everything else. It was that simple. Yet there I was, breaking and throwing one of the few unspoken laws of our family in her face. And it hurt her.

And then her own anger came seething forward.

"You know what, David? I hate you too! I hate who you have become! I don't even recognize you anymore! I don't understand what happened to you! You are not my son anymore!"

The blackness took me for the final time that day.

I remember running past her and up the stairs to my room. I remember crying and throwing things, ripping posters off my walls. I remember taking swigs out of a bottle and my throat burning with fire and flame. I remember writing in my journal, tears falling as the words poured out of me. Then, I remember reaching for the knife.

III

The first thing I was aware of when I woke was the pain. My arm ached. It was pressed against my chest and I had to peel it away from me. The lamp in my room was still on and its light revealed three fresh cuts. They were deep and, as they were freed from my shirt, they began to bleed again. It was the deepest I had ever gone.

I grabbed a handful of tissues and began dabbing at the blood. Pain shrieked up my arm. I tried hard not to moan. I picked up the bottle of vodka with a shaking hand and took a large swig. I grimaced and looked down at myself. I had bled a lot. My shirt was completely ruined. I took it off, careful so the fabric didn't touch my arm. I had started keeping band aids and bandages in my room at that point and began to wrap my arm with a white strip of bandage. I could already see the red bleeding through the white of the bandage, they looked like horrible tally marks.

***

David paused. "Would you like to hear that entry?" He asked, holding the journal. He hadn't put it down since the last time he read from it.

"I would," Lily said, "but I have a question first."

"Yeah, okay." David shrugged.

Lily sat forward a little. "When you say this," she made a motion with her pen to her clipboard, "darkness, or blackness would come, what exactly do you mean? Could you describe it a little more?"

David shifted uncomfortably in his seat for the hundredth time that day. "Uh, yeah, sure. I... well..." He thought for a moment. "You know how I was having a hard time remembering anything at first? How it was all so foggy?" Lily nodded. "Well, that's just it. Those memories, everything I've told you so far, they were foggy, or whatever. I didn't want to think about them, but once we sat down and started talking about them, a lot of them came back. When I say darkness or blackness, I honestly can't remember what happened. No matter how hard I try. There's no fog, there's just nothing. Sometimes maybe little glimpses of things. But that's about it."

Lily scribbled another note, and said, "Thank you. Okay, I'm ready for the entry."

David opened the journal. He scanned the first couple lines and let out a slow breath. "Dear god, here we go."

Dear whoever,

I have been betrayed. By my own friends. The people I loved most of all. I cannot love them anymore. I cut them out of my life to save them from myself. But now, the only thing I cut is me. I can no longer feel my soul. No one wants me. My one solace was college and they too have realized that I am no good. Unworthy. I don't know what to do. All I do is cry and lie. That's all I am. I am nothing. Today, Charlie the betrayer told me that my mother loved me. I didn't realize it but they lied to me too. My life is full of lies. When I got home, finally, there was truth. My mom, my own mother, told me she hated me. Her words ring in my head. I could see hatred in her eyes, feel the disappointment in her stare... After those words came out of her mouth, all hope for me was lost. I am filled with so much hate. I will never be happy. Hatred is the only thing that is inside of me. Hatred and emptiness. The kiss of a blade calls to me.

My sister is the only person I can find love for. The last thing I ever would want to do is to hurt her. She is so strong. She is stronger than me. I think the same demon that is taking me will come for her, and I know she will defeat it. Do what I cannot. It is going to take me. I just hope she doesn't miss me when I'm gone. I hope no one does. I don't deserve tears. I have already cried enough of them. I hope I simply fade into nothingness, the same nothingness that fills me now.

DG

David closed the journal gently. He knew would have to open it again, but he just needed it closed for the moment.

"Yikes," choked out. "So yeah, that was my very bad day and how it ended. Good times..." He glanced at the window and took a deep breath. "I knew there was something about my sister in there, but I didn't really know what it was."

"Why do you think you included her?" Lily asked. "What do you mean when you wrote," she glanced at her notes, "the same demon that is taking me will come for her?"

David shrugged. "Well, if I had to guess, it probably means that I thought she had depression too. Since that is the common theme here..." he trailed off. "I don't know how I would know that though. I honestly don't remember her that much when it was all happening. But I always knew she was there. She was there, watching, checking in on me. I think, if anything, she understood me most of all."

"Typically, people become depressed through either a triggering event or genetically. But that's not always the case. Sometimes people become depressed for no reason at all. That's just how delicate our brain chemistry is. But a huge factor is always a person's environment." Lily looked at her notes and tapped her clipboard with her pen. "So, you thought your sister had depression?"

"Lily, I don't know. I mean I guess so... I don't remember writing any of this. If I saw this shit and didn't know I wrote it, I would say some crazy person wrote it. Which is true in this case."

"David," Lily said, "you weren't crazy. You were depressed and needed help. The—"

David cut her off. "Yes, yes. I know. I'm just saying," he sighed. "Wow, this sucks." He rubbed his face and leaned back in his chair. "But we are finally at the end."

"About what your mother said, David. You know she didn't mean those words."

David grabbed his water from the floor and took a sip. "Oops, got some tears in my water. Yum." He set the cup back down. "I know. Now at least. And I don't hate her..."

"She was so scared, David. She was blinded by her own fear of what was happening to you and her own frustration in not knowing how to help you. I've spoken to your parents." Lily looked intently at David. "You need to know that."

David felt his heart lurch. He knew she was right. He knew... But it hurt all the same. "Let's just finish."

Lily looked pained and opened her mouth to say something but closed it when she saw David's expression. He held a grim determination.

"How close are we?" Lily asked.

"Well," David said, "I'm just going to brush over some things real quick. Like prom, like graduation. And yes, against all odds, I did manage to graduate. Barely. I don't even know how to be honest. Towards the end, everything is so much spottier. I'll just tell you what I do actually remember." ▢

THE END

Those last three cuts sustained me and time seemed to race by. Prom came and went. I think I was the only senior ever to be grounded for their senior prom. My mom didn't come for pictures. She just warned me of the consequences of not coming home immediately after it was over. My dad showed up for the pictures though and was almost as uncomfortable as I was. I went with Taylor, and Mike brought Ashley. After prom, we stayed out late and of course I was in trouble when I got home.

Besides prom, I had skipped everything else that I possibly could: Leland's final debate, every one of Charlie's soccer games and our class's senior banquet night. It all blurred together and I felt like instead of living, I was just waiting and only pretending to be alive.

In our final weeks of SLAM, I participated because I had too, but never once did I Leland or Charlie get me alone or, never once did I let them talk to me directly—not on the bus on the way to our final service project, not on the beach as we picked up trash, and not as we ate shitty BBQ afterwards.

Despite skipping classes, not doing any of my homework, not studying for any tests and submitting incomplete, unedited papers, I honestly had no idea how I graduated. At that point, it didn't make a difference to me.

At graduation, only my dad and brother came—my sister was home with my mom. After the ceremony, Mike and I took pictures with the rest of the Day Drinkers (they came to watch and cheer us on when we walked) and I pretended that I was happy, that I was "so happy to be done with high school" like everyone else was. But I really didn't care.

At one point, Eva tried to come up to me but I just walked away. It was the first time I had remembered seeing her in what seemed like months. I couldn't face her. I walked away from Leland and Charlie too. I still resented them for going to Mr. Holden and talking to my mother.

In a last-ditch effort, I wrote to my college. I guess there was still a small part of me that still believed that I could make it there. I wrote the administration office a letter, begging them to reconsider. I put more effort into it that I thought was possible. At that point, I had a vague understanding of what depression was and I told them how it affected my grades and blah, blah, blah. I sent it and then forgot about it, knowing that they would never reconsider. I didn't even know why I did it. I was a complete waste of time.

After I sent that letter, I waited. Not for a response, but for the clouds to come back. I wasn't happy and I wasn't bad, but I was in a perpetual state of not feeling. I didn't even argue with my mom at that point. I didn't see any reason to. All that had needed to be said between her and I had already been spoken, been shouted.

I knew I was going to kill myself. It was something I had researched online. I could feel the effects of the last time I cut slowly wearing off. What an evil thing it was. I wanted to die but I needed those black clouds and its darkness to come back to me. I finally embraced the thing that I hated most in the world: my depression-- which I thought was me--my true self revealing itself. In preparation, I wrote goodbye letters while I still could think, knowing that when it came for me, I wouldn't be able to even pretend to show compassion for anyone. Most of them were for the Day Drinkers who supported me throughout the past few months. My sister got one and so did my brother. I even tried writing my parents one. But each time I tried, I couldn't. Deep inside of me, I still wanted to love them, but I simply didn't have the capacity anymore.

Finally, the clouds blocked out the sun and the darkness came back to me. It was terrifying, but I knew it was what I needed to finish what I'd started. When I was crying myself to sleep consecutive nights, I knew I was getting close. When I heard that voice inside my head, I knew it was almost time. I wanted to die, I thought I needed too. Life was just too painful, and death... well it seemed like the only way to stop the pain. For me, for my friends, for my family. All I did was hurt and I needed to be stopped. It was the only way to part those terrible clouds forever and for everyone.

The end was so blurry. I don't know what exactly happened. I remember Leland, Charlie and Eva showing up to my house. It seemed so random. I hadn't spoken to them for so long. I was in my room when they knocked. When I opened the door and saw them standing there, in my house. I didn't know what to do. They kept telling me that they loved me and that they were so worried about me. I remember yelling at them—telling them to leave and never come back. They were so hurt. Leland and Eva were crying. But they left, eventually.

When they were gone, I rushed downstairs and found my parents in the living room.

"What did you say to them?!" I screamed. "Why were they here?! What did you tell them!?"

Then I remember running back to my room. I remember pouring pills into my mouth. I remembered my journal and frantically and viciously writing in it. I remember the knife. I remember the pain as I ripped into my arm for one final time. I remembered lying in bed and texting Eva something. I remember drifting off to sleep, waiting for the end. I remember the door breaking in and seeing them. Charlie, Leland and Eva. They had come back. They looked like angels. And then nothing.

II

Four days later, Lily walked into David's room. He was standing and looking out the window.

It took two days for the supervisor to clear David and another two days for David to want to leave. He needed recovery time. When he finished telling Lily what happened, he had begun crying uncontrollably for hours. Lily had spent the rest of her day with him. He didn't want to read the last journal entry. When she asked if she could read it, he told her no, saying, "That one belongs to me."

Lily came to check in on him throughout the next days which didn't bother him. David knew he had done what he needed to do and it was nice to have her say hi. Lily's supervisor came and gave him an evaluation. She diagnosed him with major depression and, after a long series of questions about Lily's notes, David was given approval to be discharged. A series of therapy sessions were already in place for him and several prescriptions recommended. The therapy was something he wanted to do and had no complaints. He realized how important it was just talking about what happened, and he could feel a weight lift from his shoulders. Eventually, he was ready to leave.

David turned as Lily walked in and smiled shyly, "Hey, Lily."

"Hey David," She said, returning a bright smile back at him. She didn't have her clipboard since there wasn't any need for it. "How are you feeling today?" She stopped in the middle of the room and looked out the window.

It was a beautiful day. A good day to leave.

"A bit nervous." David said, looking out the window too, and then back at her. "But, it's time. Gotta get out of this... hellhole," he chuckled and Lily joined in.

"Oh yes, what a terrible place this is. That smell is driving me crazy."

David smiled at her again, a real genuine smile. His muscles were not used to it and felt strange with the foreign movement. But it was a good feeling—like stretching your legs after sitting down for a long period of time. And then he laughed. David forgot how nice it was to really laugh. It almost made him tear up again.

"Actually," David answered, "I don't think I mind the smell anymore." His small bag with his few belongings sat on the bed, ready and waiting. He walked and picked it up. "I guess this is it."

"I guess so," Lily nodded. "Your dad is ready for you whenever you are. He's in the downstairs lobby."

"Would you like to show me out?"

"It would be my honor."

They walked down the hall together, they didn't speak, they just walked. When they reached the elevator, Lily pushed the down button.

"Did you tell my parents everything?" David asked, not looking at her.

"They know what happened, David," Lily offered and then added, "They understand."

David didn't say anything as they both walked into the elevator. It descended and when the doors to the elevator opened, the two stepped out onto the first floor. When they neared the lobby area, David stopped. Lily turned and looked at him.

"Thank you for everything, Lily." he said. "I know you were only doing your job but thank you. You're amazing."

"May I have a hug goodbye?" she asked. In response, David held out his arms and they embraced. "I'm gonna miss you. Don't ever be afraid to ask for help, David."

"I won't. Don't worry," David said as they stepped away from each other. He turned and took a deep breath. Around the corner, freedom and everything that came with it waited for him. "I think I got it from here." Lily smiled and nodded at him.

Before he could make it more than 10 feet however, Lily called to him.

"Yeah, Lily?"

"Time is a great healer. It can heal almost anything. If things are too much when you get back, just give it some time. Eventually they will heal. Things will get better."

"Thanks, Lily. You make sure Steve knows how lucky he is to have you."

"Oh," Lily said, grinning, "he does, don't you worry."

And with that, David turned and headed towards freedom.

A NEW ENDING

I

On the car ride home, David's dad began to cry.

"I'm so sorry, David. I'm sorry for being a bad father."

"Dad..." David said, trying to fight through his own tears. "Dad, you're not a bad father. You're an amazing one. I couldn't have asked for a better dad than you. I love you."

When they arrived home, David's dad didn't go inside with him, instead, he had hugged David, got back in the car and drove off, claiming that he needed to pick up some groceries.

David walked through the threshold of his house. He heard footsteps sound above him and he started to feel nauseous. Down the stairs, down the hall, around the corner... His mother walked into the kitchen and stopped as soon as she saw him. They stared at each other for a long moment, not moving, not speaking, barely breathing. Then, she walked to him and swept him into a hug, sobbing as she did so.

"I love you so much. I am so, so sorry. I love you so much."

David didn't move. He let her hug him. Then, he began crying too. It was the first time he had hugged her in months. He wrapped his arms around her and they held each other tightly, shoulders wet from the other's tears. Pain shot up his left arm but he didn't care. He needed to hold his mother and be held by her.

David finally pulled away and wiped his eyes, his mom doing the same.

"Mom... I just, I'm so sorry--"

"No," she said, cutting him off, "none of that." Her voice was serious as she grabbed his shoulders and looked him in the eyes. "I was told everything. I am so sorry I wasn't there for you. I am so sorry I couldn't help you. I am so lucky to still have you, David."

"I would have hated me too," David whispered, looking away,

feeling more tears coming. He felt like he was coming undone, like all the ropes of stress, anger, and pain finally unraveling themselves inside of him. It was slightly painful but it felt natural, it felt necessary.

"David, look at me," his mom said firmly and David did. "I never hated you. Never. Not for a second." She pulled him close to her once again. "I was just so scared. I love you so much. And nothing is ever going to change that."

"I love you, mom." David choked out the words between sobs.

When they collected themselves, they laughed together, relief flooding out of them. The war finally was over.

She took him up to his room. The floors were newly carpeted and new sheets lined the bed—David's blood having ruined the old ones.

"I have a surprise for you, David," His mom said excitedly. David raised an eyebrow at her as she reached in her back pocket and pulled out an envelope. She handed it to him and stepped away.

David looked at it, confused. "What is it?"

"Read it, David. Just read it."

He looked at the front of it. It was from his college. He hesitantly opened it and pulled out the piece of paper. He read it and looked up. "I don't understand."

"David," his mom said, "they decided to let you back in." She gave a little laugh and grabbed his shoulders. "You're going to college!"

II

Two weeks later, David found himself walking down the stairs of his house. It was a beautiful summer day and he had a doctor's appointment. He was getting his stitches out. Before he reached the kitchen, he heard his mom's voice and stopped. She sounded furious. It took him a second to realize that she was on the phone with someone.

"...He is just goddamn great. Tried to take his own life, but besides that just fucking great. You know what, Kevin?" David thought he recognized the name but didn't know who she was talking to. "Every day I wake up thinking about how the hell you have your job. You are supposed to be a professional. You are a guidance counselor!" And then it clicked, she was talking to Mr. Holden, his old guidance counselor. "When my son was at this school, did you guide him? Yes, yes, I'd say you did. Right under the rug. His friends went to you for help! I went to you for help! And what did you do? You played off his sadness, his depression, his suicidal thoughts with the word senioritis. Senioritis! You pretended that what he was doing and going through was just a nasty case of wanting to be done with high school! But what happened isn't *normal,* or something *everyone goes through*! My child came into school with bandages on his arm, and you brushed it off like harming yourself is a common thing for high schoolers to do! You are supposed to be trained! You are supposed to be able to prevent these things from happening! But instead you brushed him off like I'm sure you do with every other student who comes into your office. Did you help him graduate? No! I did! I was down on my hands and knees begging his teachers! Did you help him when his friends came to you and told you that he was hurting himself? NO! I am lucky to still have my son, Mr. Holden. I suggest you reevaluate how you want to guide your students from now on. I am sure as hell not letting you near my daughter. How dare you ask about my son! How dare you. How dare you!" David heard her stifle a sob. "Please never speak to Steph or ask about David again. Make sure her damn schedule is here this week. I never want to see or hear from you again."

David heard her slam the phone down and the soft sounds of

her sobs. He walked into the kitchen.

She was leaning against the kitchen table with her hand over her mouth, her eyes streaming with tears. When she saw David, she quickly wiped away her tears and straightened up. "Hi honey," she said, clearing her throat. "Sorry for the noise, I was just trying to get Steph's school schedule mailed. You ready to go?"

David didn't answer. He walked over and hugged her.

She had never given up on him and she never would. He realized this as a complete and undeniable fact now. Despite not knowing what was happening, despite her fear and her frustration and all her anger towards David and herself, she had never stopped trying to help, had never stopped loving him. He felt another pair of arms go around him and his mom as his dad joined in. They were his parents and he was their son. It was simple as that. No matter what, that would never change. Their love for him and his love for them would always be there. Always.

David's mom insisted on taking him to the doctors herself but upon seeing his unwrapped arm, she couldn't bear the sight and had to leave the room. David told her that it was okay. He and the doctor sat in the room together as each stitch was removed one by one from his healing arm.

Later that night, David knocked on Steph's door.

"Hey, Dave," Steph said with a smile. She was laying on her bed with her laptop sitting in front of her. "What's up?"

"Hey," he said a bit awkwardly, "I could really use your help."

David and Steph were driving to a party. David had the top down and a warm summer wind washed over him. Mike had called him. He had heard what happened and he and the Day Drinkers were eagerly waiting for David at his house. The only reason why David was going was because his new therapist, Tammy, thought it was a good idea. David had seen her twice a week after he was discharged. He liked her. She called him out on his shit. She was feisty and told him how she saw it straight up. She had told him that his depression wasn't going to go away easily, that it was going to be a constant fight but with the proper help, it was going to be manageable. Together, she and David came up with several ways to identify when a wave of depression was coming and even more ways to cope with it it, to fight it off, to stick David's mental middle finger up to it and tell it to fuck off. She even phrased it exactly like that. He liked her a lot.

During the days he was not in therapy, he took time to get back to where he once was. He had started exercising again, he wasn't drinking, was eating plenty of healthy foods and was getting more than three hours on average of sleep each night. He was even using scar cream on his arm to help the scars fade.

It was weird being back, but a good weird. His family gave him the courtesy of not speaking about anything that had happened. The past was behind them and they shut the door and threw away the key. David and his mom hung out, talked and even laughed together.

David's mental health still wasn't perfect but now that he knew what the hell was happening, he felt like he could live again. He couldn't remember being happier or closer with his family.

David thought about all this as he drove. He and Steph laughed out loud when he realized that this was probably the first time he was driving to Mike's house when he wasn't grounded. Or at least the first time since his New Year's party. That memory brought him up short.

He knew they were there waiting for him. Not the Day Drinkers, though they were there, but *them*. His best friends. Charlie, Leland and Eva. They wanted to see him, but he had refused them until now. It took a lot of convincing—Tammy led the charge. It wasn't that he didn't want to see them, because of course he did, it was the fact that he was so unbearably humiliated, so embarrassed, and so ashamed. What do you even say to someone who helped to save your life? Especially when you went out of your way to hurt them and cut them from that life... What could he possibly say to them? A mere thank you would never be enough.

David parked his car and sat there. After a while, Steph turned to him. "David, it's gonna to be okay. You got this." Together, their doors clicked open.

They walked to the front door and up the three stairs of the landing. David knocked and stepped back. He took a deep breath and Steph put a hand on his shoulder. The door opened and he saw them. His three friends that never gave up on him. They were there, all smiling, all ready, all loving. David smiled back and stepped inside.

The Mother Fucking End.

THIS BOOK IS DEDICATED TO

To my family and friends who never gave up and never stopped trying to
help

AFTERWORD

Thank you so much for reading my very first book! It might not have been the most fun read in the world but I hope that if you did manage to make it through, depression makes at least a little more sense now. To be clear, this story does not speak for all depression. This story is about my own depression. Unfortunately, depression is unique to the individual and manifests in many different ways so if you have depression or know someone who does, it might look different. If I wasn't clear in the book, don't hurt yourself, don't try to kill yourself. Understand that depression isn't your true voice and please, for the sake of the people in your life who love you, just don't. Do whatever it takes to reclaim your voice.

Special thanks to Abbie Waite and Shannon Greenhaus for helping me finish this book. Finally.

RESOURCES

NATIONAL SUICIDE PREVENTION LIFELINE:
1-800-273-8255

CRISIS TEXT LINE:
TEXT HOME TO 741741

SUICIDE & DEPRESSION CRISIS LINE-COVENANT HOUSE:
1-800-999-9999

NATIONAL YOUTH CRISIS SUPPORT:
1-800-448-4663 OR 1-800-422-0009

Made in the USA
Coppell, TX
01 December 2020